Razorback

Bedside Books
An imprint of American Book Publishing
American Book Publishing
P.O. Box 65624
Salt Lake City, UT 84165
www.american-book.com
Printed in the United States of America on acid-free paper.

Razorback

Designed by Michael Knight, design@american-book.com

Publisher's Note: *This is a work of fiction. Names, characters, places, and incidents either are the product of the author's imagination, or are used fictitiously, and any resemblance to actual persons, living or dead, events, or locales is entirely coincidental.*

ISBN 1-58982-204-8

Wilde, Scott, Razorback

Special Sales

These books are available at special discounts for bulk purchases. Special editions, including personalized covers, excerpts of existing books, and corporate imprints, can be created in large quantities for special needs. For more information
e-mail orders@american-book.com, 801-486-8639.

Razorback

By Scott Wilde

To my son Bryan,
who challenged me to write a thriller novel
and who unrelentingly read over my shoulder,
cheering me on to completion.

Foreword

Razorback, as you will soon discover, is a unique and compelling thriller whose suspense immediately drew me in. Once I started, I found the book difficult to put down. Mr. Wilde has beautifully integrated fact and fiction into an informative and entertaining read. Anyone, friend or foe of feral hogs, will find this book a worthwhile investment of their time.

Being familiar with the area where the story unfolds and having grown up on a cattle operation, I found it easy to relate to Mr. Wilde's descriptions of the local flora and fauna, community settings and activities, and ranch life; right down to the chores and Sunday dinners. Mr. Wilde has masterfully woven in factual information about feral hog biology, habitat preferences, and their effects on other wildlife species and the environment. The fictional insertions describing attacks on humans and the dietary preference of the giant razorback, "Ol' Lucifer," certainly spices up the thriller component of the book. Feral hogs are found in many states in the U.S. and, where present, can have devastating effects on farming, ranching, and the local environment. Being opportunistic omnivores, feral hogs have been known to destroy riparian or wetland areas, agricultural crops, and pastures for livestock. Also, they are not beyond killing young wildlife and livestock in their foraging routines. Many stories of their aggressive nature have been told among those who hunt these animals. These activities have relegated them to being the bane of wildlife managers, farmers, ranchers, landowners, and environmentalists.

About the only practical means of controlling the feral hog population are shooting and trapping. Mr. Wilde's references to hunting feral hogs with dogs and trapping accurately reflect enjoyable pursuits created by the hogs' presence. The inundation of the local area by hunters wanting to shoot Ol' Lucifer, although fictional, is still a good reflection of the popularity of hunting feral hogs. Some farmers and ranchers have decided to make the best of a bad situation by selling hog hunts to interested hunters. In many cases, selling feral hog hunts provides much needed income to farmers and ranchers, and pumps money into rural economies through lodging, food, and gas revenues.

Whether you like them or hate them, feral hogs have demonstrated that they can adapt to just about any habitat type or region. Fortunately or unfortunately, when they appear in an area, they are likely to be there for a while unless drastic measures are taken early to eliminate them. If you discover feral hogs in your area, you can obtain factual information about them from your state wildlife department, or local university extension and Natural Resources Conservation Service offices.

In the meantime, sit back and enjoy *Razorback* for the thriller novel that it is. I hope that you enjoy it as much as I did.

Russell Stevens

Russell Stevens is a wildlife and range specialist with the Samuel Roberts Noble Foundation in Ardmore, Oklahoma. He holds a master of science degree in Animal Science, Range and Wildlife option. He is certified as a wildlife biologist by the Wildlife Society and is certified as a range management consultant and certified professional in rangeland management by the Society for Range Management.

Stevens receives numerous inquiries each month regarding information about feral hogs. He also consults with farmers and ranchers as well as landowners regarding feral hogs. He has authored and co-authored several agriculturally related publications including: *The Feral Hog in Oklahoma, Quality of Native Plant Forage Species Important to White-tailed Deer and Goats in South Central Oklahoma, Plant Image Gallery*, a web-based pictorial guide to identifying grasses, forbs, and woody plants, and *Grasses of Southern Oklahoma and North Texas: a Pictorial Guide.*

Chapter One

In my dreams, I run in total terror as the wild boar demons chase me through the misty gray scenes in my mind until I am face-to-face with the devil boar charging straight at me. I can hear his bloodcurdling squeal and smell his stench as he lunges at me, flailing his head back and forth, struggling to reach me with those deadly, razor-sharp tusks.

Only now, after so many years, do I have the courage to relive those days and tell my story of the deadly hogs in its entirety.

As I sit on the Trinity Rail Express commuter train from Fort Worth to Dallas, where I work, I stare out at the raindrops moving diagonally across the window as we rhythmically rock along the tracks. It is still so dark that all I really see is my own reflection staring back. The hour-long trip each day provides me the time to contemplate and vividly recall the sweet and bitter events of my life in 1973.

I live in Fort Worth now, and I don't regret for a moment leaving the East Texas Piney Woods. I am an editor and columnist for the *Dallas Morning News*; a job that has taken me from writing about politics to reading everyone's take on current news stories. My column provides me a forum to declare the ludicrousness of society's debates over issues that occupy bored minds when truly serious issues, such as dealing with wars and rumors of wars, are not available.

I moved from East Texas thinking I was leaving the horrible experience of 1973 behind. I used my GI bill to get through college and subdue the memories of the loss of my father and brother. But, only time and God can heal. There was once a time I couldn't say that.

My name is William "Billy" Longbow. My great-papa was Chickasaw Indian from Oklahoma. He married an Irish girl; that's another story. I grew up ten miles outside of Lufkin, Texas, near the Angelina River on a 7,680-acre ranch. My pa's forefathers cleared parts of the land just after 1845 when the U.S. annexed Texas. Ma and Pa, Rose and Jack Sr. respectively, had two sons: Jack Junior and me. Jack, or JJ as we always called him, was two years older than me. He was always the biggest boy in his class; a little on the heavy side, but it sure didn't slow him down. We both got Ma's fair skin, but he had coal-black hair like Pa and I have medium-brown hair like Ma. I was leaner and destined not to be as tall as JJ. While I was in the upper middle of my class most of the time, JJ wouldn't settle down enough from hunting and riding horses to take school seriously. Funny thing, JJ could grow a beard at fourteen, but it didn't ever grow in thick, even to his last days; yet I sport a heavy mustache.

As soon as JJ was old enough to hold a rifle, he discovered his love for hunting. When the chores were done, Pa would let us go exploring. I never liked to hunt, but I loved exploring with my big brother. We'd head straight for the corral and saddle up our horses. They loved it too. As soon as we opened the gate they were chomping at the bit to run into the woods. Winnie May, JJ's dark brown quarter horse, was high-spirited. She was a dangerous mare under most people, but acted well under JJ. I guess she had enough two-by-fours across the nose. My horse, Rounder, was a paint. He was a fifteen-year-old gelding and would let a baby guide him around. Pa always wanted to breed Winnie May, so she stayed high-spirited and was never fixed. As for Rounder, he lost his manhood years ago. I guess he decided he didn't have anything to prove anymore.

JJ always pretended that he didn't want me along until we got to the woods. He always took his .22-caliber rifle and talked about how he could feed the whole family if we needed him to. For as long as I knew, he was a dead aim. Once, I challenged him to take down a doe at sixty yards by shooting her in the eye and into her brain. To prove how good he was, he did it. I was totally amazed and disgusted, which officially made me a wimp in his eyes. I would chase down his animals for him, but I always felt remorse when I'd come up on a bird or a squirrel lying senselessly dead. Although JJ wouldn't admit it, I could tell he felt it too sometimes; but his sense of identity and instinct to feed our family overruled any remorse he may have felt.

Although I didn't want to kill anything, I still wanted to

learn some of JJ's hunting skills. He taught me how to skin the critters and dress them to bring home. Ma had long since learned how to cook a variety of game stews and casseroles. It sure helped out on our meager budget. The cattle business was always up and down. So Pa worked as a mechanic in town to subsidize our income while Ma worked part-time cleaning houses for doctors and lawyers.

Ma always made us slick up on Sunday morning and go to church. Pa never went. He said he had too much catching up to do around the farm. Our preacher, Reverend Durham, was a tall man with a fair complexion. Like JJ, he loved to hunt too, and would incorporate his hunting experiences into his sermons. He had been to Africa on missions and had been on safaris while he was there. I could tell JJ was spellbound when the reverend would tell his stories. Ma had found them atrocious. She said he was misusing church funds. I always thought he just used his own money.

I clearly remember when I was eleven, the day when Reverend Durham came to church on Sunday with his right hand heavily bandaged in white gauze and first-aid tape. He had been hunting hogs that week on horseback with another member of our congregation, Sam Kinkade. Sam was a big, middle-aged cowboy with a large, gray handlebar mustache. He never went anywhere without his spurs on, even to church. We used to tease him about how he dressed like he had just stepped out of a cowboy movie. He wasn't from East Texas originally; he moved from Wichita Falls about ten years earlier and bought a big ranch near Lufkin. He was a lighthearted man who liked to joke and, in spite of how we used to kid him, he was a great cowboy and a national champion team roper. JJ was always polite when Sam was around, because he admired him so much. Of course, it didn't hurt that JJ also had a crush on Sam's daughter, Annie.

Sam took the reverend out often and let him observe the hunt from behind. This time, the reverend convinced Sam to let him take part in the action and hog-tie a 150-pound boar when the dogs had him subdued. Sam warned him to keep his hands away from the boar's head. The reverend tied up its back legs, flipped him over, and in his excitement, reached for the hog's front legs without paying attention. In that fraction of a second, the dog quit pulling in order to get a better bite on the ear and the boar turned his head, snapped off the reverend's pointer finger and swallowed it.

Reverend Durham saw the blood, turned sheet white, and fainted. Sam killed the boar, then had to drag the reverend back to the pickup after he wrapped his hand. He gathered his dogs and got the reverend to the emergency room.

That Sunday, everyone was entertained, especially the kids, because that was the finger the reverend used to point at us with when he was telling us how "You're goin' to hell if you don't repent now! Get on your knees and plead to Jesus for mercy!" Now, he would have to point at us with his middle finger and look like he was flipping off everyone.

That day, I remember, he preached about the demons that will torment you worse than those cold-eyed devil hogs out there.

I remember Sister Sally Durham, the reverend's wife,

was ranting, raving, and carrying on all the day long about her husband's despicable hunting hobby. "He spends all our money and all his extra time out there chasing around the woods like some bloodthirsty Neanderthal. Heaven forbid, we all know the commandment, 'Thou Shalt Not Kill,' but they don't think that applies to animals 'cause they don't have spirits. Then he gets his finger bit off!"

I remember how her statement about animals had affected me as a kid. How could animals not have spirits? They're alive, they move, and think too, and God created them just like he did us.

That afternoon, JJ, our friend Grant from church, and I ran home, changed our clothes, went straight to the barn and saddled up Winnie May and Rounder. Grant hopped up on Rounder with me and we ran the horses through the open pasture avoiding the well-known wet spots that we had been dumped in before and headed for the edge of the woods. We rode until we came to the familiar white sycamore tree. There, we followed a deer trail into the woods to the creek we named Longbow Creek because it ran through our property. The creek was a tributary to the Angelina River. On a bend in the creek, there was a rocky outcrop JJ and I enjoyed going to. We tied up the horses a ways back, then walked to the outcrop and sat where we could see the creek through the trees and watch the wildlife. We threw rocks as far as we could to try to hit some of the persistent pools, and we talked.

"Ol' Reverend Durham's purty funny, ain't he," said JJ.

Grant and I chuckled. "Yep, I guess he's got more respect for razorbacks now, don't he," said Grant.

"Yeah. I heard about that dog huntin' for wild boars. That sounds purty cool, but you gotta be careful. They say if you're not, the hogs will end up huntin' you," said JJ. He paused, pondering something. "When I get older, I wanna be a huntin' guide. Ya think Pa will let us bring customers onto our property to help bring in a little cash? We got a lotta deer and hogs here."

"I don't know, JJ, he's awful particular 'bout his privacy." I paused, absorbing the beautiful day, then spoke again. "You know, I love bein' out here in the woods as much as you do, but why do you wanna kill everything? I think animals got spirits too, just like humans. When I watch any animal, like birds and cottontails or deer and horses, they all have different personalities just like people. I think when God said, 'Thou shalt not kill,' he meant the needless killin' of anything," I exclaimed, knowing I'd get JJ riled up.

"Billy, that just ain't the way I see it. The Bible don't teach that animals have spirits. We humans are predatory animals. It's just our nature. That's why Reverend Durham preaches every Sunday then hunts all week. I'm fixin' to take advantage of that nature by bein' a guide and helpin' people satisfy that need," he said, looking at me with an authoritative smile.

"JJ, there's just one thing wrong with your theory. I ain't driven to hunt, and I'm a human too."

"Look guys!" he blurted out, ignoring my argument.

I looked where he was pointing and saw five wild hogs working their way along the riparian area on the other side of the creek bend and rocky outcrop we were sitting on.

"Wow, I didn't know we had that many wild hogs 'round here," I said, trying to keep track of them through the trees.

"I knew they were here. I seen their scat and some places where they been rootin' along the creek."

"Well, I ain't seen any of their tracks before," said Grant curiously.

"Me neither," I said.

"You just didn't know what you been lookin' at. They're all over along our fence lines where they're lookin' for an easy way to get in," he said.

"Shh! Look!" I said, pointing deeper into the woods.

"Wow! Billy, that boar's a monster. He's the biggest one I ever seen—even at the state fair! He's gotta be as big as a cow."

We held still as statues and watched as he rooted and snorted through the woods. Then he stopped and stuck his snout in the air in our direction, made a quick shuffle around to face us and snorted a few times. We could see his snout wriggling as he checked the air.

"He's on to us. He caught our scent," JJ whispered without moving a muscle.

The boar put his head down and waved it from side to side, snorting a couple times and waving tusks that had to be six inches long. As quickly as he did, he wheeled around and disappeared. Amazingly, we didn't hear a sound.

Once we were sure he was gone, JJ spoke up, "He looked different than the others. I never seen one a solid silvery black with longer hair like that. I think he was one of them Russian boars I hear people talkin' about. I never thought they were that big."

Without saying a word, I looked at JJ who was still staring into the woods where the boar disappeared. I could tell his heart was beating as fast as mine.

When it looked clear, Grant turned to us. "Let's go take a look at the tracks," he suggested.

"I don't think that's such a good idea. Those hogs could still be down there," I said.

"Come on Billy, those hogs are long gone. And even if they weren't, they'd be gone when they hear us crashing around down there. Besides, I'm a deadly aim with this .22," said JJ.

Grant led the way and found a shallow spot in the creek. We took our shoes off and crossed over. It wasn't hard to find the tracks.

"They look a lot like deer tracks to me," I said.

"The cloven hooves are spread apart more, and they look rounder than deer; and look, here's what their scat looks like," said JJ pointing out the differences to us.

"It looks almost like human's," said Grant.

"Yeah, or a little clumpy, dependin' on what they ate," continued JJ.

I was amazed at my big brother. He seemed to know everything. I was proud to be around him.

We followed the tracks to where the big one came onto the trail. His tracks were deeper in the mud and more than twice the size of the others.

"Wow, this one's a bruiser," I exclaimed.

We were talking away when something caught our attention. We all stopped and looked at each other. With our noses wrinkled and a curious look on our faces, we sensed a foul odor that smelled like a decaying carcass. In a fraction of a moment, I heard a snap behind Grant and looked just in time to see the huge boar standing with his head down. He expelled a blood-curdling squeal and charged with his head down, coming through the woods straight for us. He looked like a locomotive on the run.

I screamed as I pointed, and then turned to run, "Hog! Hog!"

I ran for my life! JJ turned around too, saw the boar, stumbled, and fell trying to make a run for it. He bounced up as fast as he went down. Grant was straight in the boar's path.

Grant looked at us in surprise, then turned to see what was behind him. Terrified, he took two steps to run away. JJ and I both stood helplessly at a distance and screamed as we watched the huge boar hook Grant by the inside of his right leg with his enormous tusk and flip him off his feet. Grant came down hands first and his legs up in the air. Blood spewed from inside his leg as he slapped the ground with a neck-wrenching thud. The boar straddled Grant's back. Grant tried to get up and crawl. A look of terror was in his eyes as he screamed for help. We stood helplessly and watched the boar step on his back and shove him to the ground. In a wild rage, the boar swung his head from side to side slashing Grant's back and sides with razor-sharp tusks. The boar squealed in fury and Grant screamed our names for help until the boar stepped on his back again, collapsing his lungs and probably snapping his spine. Grant let out a horrible grunt. Blood spewed from his mouth. He quivered a little, and that was the end. The boar came around to Grant's side and rolled him over with his tusks. He continued to slash his belly open, rapidly flailing his huge head side to side. Blood and body parts spewed everywhere, and Grant's intestines rolled out. The stench of open bowels permeated the air. The boar turned his rear end to us and quieted down to irregular grunts as he nudged Grant to confirm the death of his prey. JJ and I climbed trees as quickly as we could.

The other hogs in the vicinity must have heard the commotion or smelled the carnage. Time slowed as we watched the huge boar and the five smaller hogs devour Grant's remains, fighting and pulling at his lifeless body parts. Those beasts ate bone and all. In a matter of minutes, only some torn clothes and bone fragments were left.

JJ and I stayed in the trees for hours after the hogs left, staring at the remains, sobbing uncontrollably, chins quivering and shivering from shock over what we had witnessed. Finally, in silence, JJ climbed down and ran to me. He grabbed my leg and pulled at me to get down.

"Come on, Billy!"

I came out of my trance, whimpered as I climbed down, and then we both ran for our lives, splashed across the creek and bolted to the horses, wondering if they were even going to be there. They were okay. We jumped on and ran those horses as hard as they would gallop back home.

The sheriff's posse and several other men from Lufkin came out on the property for weeks after the incident. They brought dogs and traps trying to capture the huge devil hog.

Grant's parents quit coming to church. I think they

blamed us for the loss of their son because they never talked to us again when we saw them around town. They told people we were a bad influence on Grant, and they never would have approved of him going out like that on Sunday. I don't remember them ever complaining when he asked them if he could. I'd get a deep wrenching feeling in my stomach as I'd watch them walk away from me, hurrying his little brother and sisters along. They'd look back at me with that unresolved question in their eyes. I wanted so badly to talk with them and cry with them for the loss of their son.

For many years thereafter, I kept silent about the issue. I would stare at the woods surrounding our property and imagine that monster out there lurking around for his next prey. I didn't want anything more to do with hunting and refused to go back into the woods. JJ was always the bold one. He started hunting again; although, he would never go alone. He had vengeance in his eyes. Even though he never said anything, everyone knew he was hoping to run into the hog again and take his anger out on it. Pa saw it in JJ when he would take him hunting, and JJ would act out his anger on any large animal that he saw. Pa tried to tell us the old hog had long since died, but JJ and I didn't believe it. We never talked about it, but I knew it bothered JJ just the same, because he would wake up screaming in the night. It wasn't until we were in high school that I would go with JJ into the woods. By then, logic overtook childish imagination most of the time. We'd go into the woods, but I still flinched at unusual sounds.

Chapter Two

I couldn't understand the logic of the draft. JJ got off on a minor technicality; he had some hearing loss in his right ear. Ma and Pa attributed it to all of JJ's hunting—shooting a rifle without earplugs. I couldn't imagine how that made any difference in war. I figured a lot of noise from airplanes, helicopters, bombs, and guns could mess up your hearing anyway, and there was no better sniper potential than JJ. After I got to Vietnam though, I understood. It takes good hearing for radio, phones, and for being in the brush and hearing what's going on around you. Bad hearing can easily get you killed.

I never liked the idea of going to fight a war in a foreign country where the people we are helping aren't even sure they want our help, but I always knew I would willingly go if I was called. Two years after JJ got out of the draft, I found myself stripped, reclothed in fatigues, shaved bald, run almost to death, and headed for Vietnam. I ended up a side gunner on a Huey 67H20 helicopter. I was scared to death at first, thinking I was hanging out there for anyone to pick off. I later changed my opinion when I realized it was that or patrolling the forests and being on the front lines in offensive strikes. At least I could see the enemy from above and shower terror down on them. Like anywhere in the war, it was a matter of seeing and shooting before they saw you and shot you. I got high on helping get our boys out of blistery hot spots. For a man who didn't like to shoot animals, I killed my fair share of Viet Cong. I did hear of many of our chopper patrols being shot down and/or the side gunners getting blown away. I had to separate myself from it; it was war.

Ma often wrote to me and told me that her daily vigil prayers kept me safe. I didn't put much stock in that. I just thought it was the luck of the draw. When someone picked my card, I'd be gone. I believed everything happened with total randomness. God didn't point his finger and say, "Okay, it's your turn to die today" or "I think I'll save you today." I believed another man's decision and being in the wrong place at the wrong time could definitely affect your outcome. That's the only thing that made sense to me as I saw one person die and another right next to him live. There didn't seem to be much picking and choosing going on.

Anyway, everyone's heard all the Vietnam stories. I won't belabor this story with the common ones. However, I do want to share my worst Vietnam experience, because it's the one that brought me home. It happened when we started getting confident with our successes. I was very close to my buddies in my patrol. We had fought and been successful for nearly nine months. This particular night, I remember I couldn't sleep. The night was sultry.

Just as I dozed, Sergeant Yankton barged in yelling, "Wake up! Let's move out!"

We jumped up and went through the same routine. As I loaded my M16, I settled myself down by thinking about other night runs we'd been on. We took off, and everyone was serious. Night just has a way of being more haunting. Talking or trying to provide comic relief was useless over the roar of the chopper.

As we flew, Sergeant Yankton explained the mission to us, yelling over the pounding of the chopper blades, "There's a patrol seven miles north in the Tsumon Highlands surrounded by VC. They found a hornet's nest. We need to take the heat off."

We flew over a little hill and into a ravine on the other side. I could hear Sergeant Yankton communicating with their patrol leader. Although I couldn't understand everything they said, I could hear the desperation in the patrol leader's voice. When we got to them, we could see them hunkered down on a terrace above the ravine. Viet Cong had them surrounded across the ravine, coming up the ravine, and coming down the slope at them. Sergeant Yankton ordered them to stay down until we could make a sweep and knock out an open spot for us to land. Our spotlights revealed VC everywhere along the edges of the dense forest. I discharged our grenade launcher at them to knock a hole in the stronghold. Their hats shown in the spotlight like little reflectors. It was easy to knock them out from above. I sprayed the area to knock them out anywhere the light shone to assure none of them shot back at us.

My stomach sickened when I saw the younger less experienced boys panicking at the edge of our lights and trying to make a run for it. Lack of communication or sheer delirium, I don't know, but they were mowed down, blood splattering from their backs, heads, and legs.

We came around for a second sweep to clear out a particular area close to the slope and as far away as possible from the ravine they were coming up. Just as we approached, a bright red-orange streak came screaming straight at us. We were too low to dodge it. It blew off the rear stabilizer prop. We went into a tailspin going down fast. The chopper hit with the left side of the nose down. I heard the chopper blades disintegrating and missile pieces whistling by. All I could think of was that I hoped the pieces were taking out as many VC as possible.

I was fortunate. My side landed up, and I was not seriously injured. Being strapped in to hang out the side of the chopper the way I was, if my side would have hit first, I would have been crushed. As it was, I took a pretty good beating, being shaken around, but I was okay. All I could think of was the VC closing in on us. I shot into the dark on either side trying to discourage them from coming. Suddenly, THUD—that sound we all knew well and hated—a bullet tearing through flesh. I looked down and could barely see the chunk taken out of my left thigh. It didn't really hurt initially; it reminded me of when I would hit the corner of my footboard with my thigh at night trying to get around the bed when I couldn't see in the dark. A second later though, the full comprehension of what just happened struck me. The excruciating burn began as cool air penetrated my wound and warm blood saturated my pants. My buddy Jake was just emerging from the wreckage, shaking off his bumps and bruises.

"Jake, I'm hit in the thigh. I don't know how bad it is," I yelled.

"Aieee, Billy, I got you," he exclaimed in his strong Cajun accent. He jumped out, grabbed my gun and sprayed out away from the stranded patrol again. Then he lay me down and packed my wound to keep me from bleeding to death. Someone yelled that Sergeant was dead. He had sustained massive head injuries and the pilot was barely alive.

Out of the darkness came several of our boys from the stranded patrol. They had broken through, thanks to us, and were cheering. Their patrol leader yelled that a backup chopper was on its way. He explained that their platoon had split up to go into these ravines, and they found the hot spot. He added that the rest of his platoon sounded safe.

Suddenly, bullets were slapping into the side of the chopper and whizzing by. The patrol leader got all his men together and surrounded us, shooting into the dark.

Finally, the other chopper arrived and I was one of the first to be loaded on. I felt guilty that I couldn't stay there to help defend the rest.

I was flown back with four wounded from my patrol and the four men from the other patrol who had carried us to the chopper. Eventually, shock and the loss of blood overtook me. I blacked out as I heard someone explaining the urgency of the situation.

When I regained consciousness, I was in the medic's tent with several other wounded soldiers. I asked questions about the rescue mission and if my patrol and the other patrol had gotten out safely. Everyone I asked acted as if they were too busy to stop and answer me. As my faculties returned, I realized that I had been out for nearly three hours.

The medic looked at me and smiled, "You're a hero, buddy. You're up for the Purple Heart and a ticket home."

It didn't sink in, and that didn't answer my question.

"Did the two patrols make it out okay?" I asked more intently.

The smile disappeared from the medic's face. "The chopper dropped you guys off and went right back. When they got there it was too late. The VC had moved in and, didn't just kill everyone, but disemboweled them to send us a message. The chopper flew over with the spotlight and the VC had moved on. We spent the night cleaning up the carnage and bringing our boys home in body bags."

"Where's Jake? Did he come with us or did he stay behind?" I asked trying to sit up.

"Was that the Cajun?"

"Yeah," I responded apprehensively.

"He fought a good fight," was all the medic would say and walked off before he had to say any more. From the look on his face, he was visibly shaken up.

I couldn't stand it. My body shuddered from head to toe, and it wasn't from the pain in my thigh. I broke into uncontrollable tears. My friends were gone. I didn't want to go home. I was so full of rage that I wanted to go back out and blow away as many VC devils as I could.

Chapter Two

The next few days were unbearable, suffering from the pain in my hip and in my heart. My only reprieve from my tormented thoughts was when Arnie, the medic, would do his rounds. He brought along his newly found pet, a twenty-pound Vietnamese Potbelly pig, which had wandered into camp. It was so ugly it was cute. It was predominately black with white patches and had a bright-pink snout. Its belly barely came off the ground. It reminded me of a low rider. I envisioned it getting high-centered trying to get over logs and rocks. The thing followed him like a faithful puppy. Arnie had taught the pig several tricks. It was a hoot to see a pig fetch, sit up, and beg.

One of the boys from the other patrol had been badly injured, shot just below the right knee. The medics had tried to get circulation back to the lower extremity but it wasn't happening. Late one night, the boy was delirious from a fever. The infection was taking over, and the doctors knew they had to take the lower leg off. They doped him up to where he couldn't feel a thing and proceeded to cut off his leg. Obviously, they weren't worried about who was watching. This was war.

The bone had been shattered and they needed to make a clean cut. There's nothing sacred or technical about the procedure. They simply pulled out a stainless steel saw and started cutting. The hacking sound on bone made me nauseous. When the lower part of the leg was off, the medics, focused on the patient, threw the leg aside in a yellow and red biohazard bucket. The can was about eighteen inches high. They went back to work. Arnie was one of the medics assisting.

While the medics intently worked on the patient, cleaning and suturing what was left of his leg, Arnie's potbellied pig made his way into the tent nosing around. No one was watching the pig but me. That little hog climbed up on the bucket, pulled the amputated limb out, and began feasting on the tattered flesh. I couldn't stand to watch that wretched animal trying to gorge itself on human flesh. I wondered how opportunistic it had been before Arnie took it in. I couldn't stand it; I yelled and pointed. A little embarrassed, Arnie looked at me then the hog, and then went over and kicked him out of the tent. He then nonchalantly picked up the severed appendage, threw it back into the bucket like a piece of garbage, and went back to work. War had desensitized these men. It was a matter of survival.

Chapter Three

I was flown back to Saigon and that was the last I saw of the war zone. Still traumatized by the thoughts of my comrades never coming home alive, I could not appreciate the fact that I was alive and was headed home early. I spent a few weeks in a military hospital in San Diego before being discharged. It takes the military a day to get you signed up and into the military, but weeks to process you out. I fought infection for a short time, but that was gone by the time I went home. I felt good—for a guy on crutches. The bullet left an ugly scar on my thigh, but left enough muscle to effectively let me walk. I was optimistic that I would only have an ugly scar and a mild limp for the rest of my life. I was a local hero for a while and was spotlighted in the paper. Whenever I went to Lufkin to run errands, someone would stop me to welcome me back or to express their opinion about the war. They expressed their ignorance most of the time. Rather than getting angry, I would walk off—

most of the time.

I remember coming home from town fuming after having a discussion with Bobby Hayden, an old friend that I had played basketball with in high school. He was probably six inches taller than me and played center in school. He saw me at a convenience store and recognized me almost immediately. He hustled over to the pump where I was getting gas. He was all excited to see me again.

"I read about you in the paper. Sorry 'bout what happened. What a waste."

"Yeah. So whatta you doin' with your life?" I asked.

"I've been goin' to Stephen F. Austin College in Nacogdoches. I'm a junior now."

"So, how did you get outta the draft?" I asked, feeling a little envious.

"Well, I got interested in the Jehovah's Witness faith and joined their beliefs. It's a shame that we got good boys over there losin' their lives in that wicked war. I feel like God has commanded us not to associate ourselves…"

Bobby had changed a lot since high school and I wasn't having any of it. I cut him off immediately; all I could think of was Pa getting all riled up when they'd come knocking on our door. He used to say he didn't have any use for a religion that didn't believe in patriotism and would not defend our God-inspired country. I figured Bobby was just easing his conscience for being too cowardly to get drafted.

I got in his face and paused for a moment, then I said with quiet intensity, "You're a coward and oughtta be thrown in jail. I hope God damns you people who hide behind him in the name of religion 'cuz you're too scared to defend your country."

I was inches from his face. Out the corner of my eye, I could see people stopping, listening, and talking about breaking this up. I looked around with fury in my eyes challenging anyone to even try. People held their ground. I looked at him again. He was shaking.

In a much louder tone, I said, "There were some devoutly religious people over there goin' to see their maker, and if there's a God, they'll be the ones by his side—not you cowards."

Bobby slowly backed off without saying a word and went into the convenience store where he was safely around other people. I could see everyone talking and questioning him. I didn't care what other people thought. My only real buddies were dead. I went back to pumping my gas so I could get out of there.

Reflecting back, I realize that he was simply stating his beliefs and was actually trying to empathize with me in his own way. I wasn't ready for that yet, but now, even though I don't necessarily agree with him, I regret the things I said to him. He had every right to his opinions. That's a right we fight for.

Although I thought I was tough, now I recognize my posttraumatic syndrome. I thought I would have nightmares for a while, then fit in; but, after several months, I still found myself most comfortable being reclusive. I could relate to no one and I was viciously jumpy. It was a visceral reaction and I warned my family not to approach me unexpectedly. It was an instinct everyone develops after spending time in the Vietnam jungles. Ma and Pa simply kept their distance, not knowing how to respond to my negativity. Talk had gotten around town and Ma and Pa had heard about my confrontation with Bobby at the convenience store. People felt uncomfortable with my parents and ostracized them, not wanting to start anything with them.

JJ was in and out at home. He had started a job with the local utility company as a lineman. He would get called out at all hours, which hadn't given us much time to talk.

After several months of dealing with my attitude, JJ saw through me. On a day when he had a little time off, he told me that he and I needed to go explore our old haunts. We walked to the barn and corral. Winnie May and Rounder were still there and looked as healthy as ever.

"Whenever I go out on Winnie May, I take Rounder with me. I can tell he missed you. He jus' looked so lonely ever since you left," he told me.

I knew he was just trying to make me feel good. It did bring a smile to my face. We saddled up and he led me to our old outpost: the rock outcrop on the bend of the creek.

As soon as he got me there, he confronted me, "You gotta get over this, Billy. Quit condemnin' others for their ignorance. They're just people. Put the war behind you. You're not goin' back. The stuff that happened there wasn't your fault. It goes way above you. Get over it and come home!"

"You need to just stay outta my life," I snapped.

With no fear, he looked at me and laughed. All of his life he could easily whip me and still thought he could. His laugh infuriated me and I went after him like a cornered wild animal as I had done many times growing up. Only this time, with my combat training, I nearly beat him sense-less. JJ screamed for me to stop. I suddenly realized what I was doing. I had unleashed my anger at Vietnam on him. I stopped before I killed him, stood down, hugged him with all my might, and began weeping bitterly. With a bloody nose and ears, and a few bruised ribs, JJ sat there and let me cry. He put his arms around me.

"Not even Pa has ever whupped me like that," he said, shaking a little. Then he laughed and wiped his nose. I laughed too. But I didn't want to let go of him. He was my big brother.

"I let my buddies down. If I hadn't gotten myself shot, I coulda stayed to help 'em and maybe someone else coulda gotten home. I never been so scared in my life as that moment," I stammered.

"Billy, Ma and Pa prayed you home. It wasn't your fault those boys got killed. Let it go!"

That was a powerful healing moment. JJ never said an-other word to me about the war and never told Ma or Pa what happened. My parents figured we were adults now and we could work out our own problems. We were close again, but with a whole different understanding.

Ma figured I had been home long enough and it was time for me to go to church with her again. She said the whole congregation, including Reverend Durham, was anx-ious for me to come back.

I knew this was going to be hard on her, but I was an adult and I had to be honest. "Ma, I love you and I hope you know that, but I have to be honest with you. I don't believe in God…"

"Oh, Son, don't start talkin' like that. It's sinful. You just need to pray and…"

"No, Ma, please don't start on me. Respect my beliefs and my stand. I won't impose it on you, so don't impose this on me. That's just the way I feel right now."

I could see the hurt in her face and I knew what she was thinking. She just knew it was God who brought me back home—how could I be so indignant? Inside, though, I couldn't imagine that a merciful God would stand back and let such good young men like my patrol buddies be massacred. Ma was hurt, but she never bothered me again.

Pa had been in the army too. He did his duty in Korea fighting in the bitter cold and watching his buddies being killed for a cause that to this day still hasn't reached a resolution. Pa never discussed it with me until a couple days after my confrontation with Ma. I guess our common experiences helped him feel like he could relate to me.

I was in the pasture with Pa helping him hook up the fertilizer spreader to the tractor. He stood and looked at me for a moment with a contemplative smile. He seemed old. His eyes were still as dark and sparkly as they always had been, but his age and years in the sun had creased his face. His face and arms were dark from the sun and his Indian heritage, but the rest of him was white. He would be fifty-one soon. His coal-black, cropped hair—a haircut he hadn't changed in twenty years—was now mostly white with a little spattering of black trying to hold out. He hadn't shaved that morning and his whiskers were as white as his hair. His hands and forearms, although showing age lines and less elasticity in his skin, looked as strong as ever, but they were connected to a chest that was not as full and barrel-looking as it had once been. He had always had a flat stomach and, although I would never kid him about it, it was getting a little rounder. Laying all this aside, he could still work me into the ground putting in long days, provided he got a short nap at lunch.

"What's the matter, Pa?" I asked, looking at him a little puzzled.

"I'm just admirin' you, Son. You looked so grown-up in your army fatigues when you went off to war. But now, I look at you and I see a fully developed and very independent man standin' before me. I wonder where the time disappeared. A man couldn't be prouder of two boys than I am of you an' JJ. The two of you sure had your spats, but overall you stayed close and I thank God for that."

This caught me by surprise. I didn't think Pa believed in God.

"You're a handsome young man, William. You look so much like your ma when she was young." Only Pa could call me William. "I imagine you and JJ will be runnin' off and gettin' married soon," he said winking at me.

I smiled back, "I don't think that's somethin' you have to worry about any time soon." I paused reflectively. "Pa, I didn't think you believed in God."

"I didn't. Just like you, I figured the preachers at church had no concept of real life out there and neither did most of the congregation. I thought they just lived in their own little perfect world, but as time went on, my heart softened. Although I still don't go to church, I've come to realize I never really didn't believe. I was just too angry to admit that it wasn't God killin' those folks. He probably weeps like the rest of us. He said the sun shines on both the wicked and the righteous. He sees his kids makin' cruel decisions to try to seek the puny power of this world by using the greatest gift he gave us: the freedom to choose right from wrong for ourselves. The old devil can take us over purty easy if we let him.

"I'd be workin' these cattle out here, prayin' ever' day for you. I promised I'd never deny him again if you made it home safely, and here you are standin' before me alive and well after bein' in the bowels of hell."

I looked at my father and realized he was a changed man in more ways than just his gray hair. "I love you, Pa, and I think you're the only person who can fully understand what I'm goin' through. Maybe someday I'll see it the way you do."

"Son, you got all the time you want. I'll be here whenever you wanna talk." He smiled at me and nodded. "Now let's get some work done around here. Day's a burnin'."

That was the last we talked about it that day. We spent the rest of the afternoon working hard—that didn't change. I went to bed as exhausted as I used to get at boot camp.

I think that was the turning point for me. After that, I don't remember ever being confrontational. I still had the bad dreams, but I didn't take it out on people anymore.

Chapter Four

In the year-and-a-half that I was in the army, JJ had convinced Pa that it would be a good source of income to start a hunting guide service on our ranch. He set out deer feeders in late summer the year before, and had been managing these strategic locations. Deer were abundant and almost domesticated near the house. Pa said the hunters had to stay a half-mile away from the house. If he saw any of them hunting or shooting within that half-mile radius, the guide service would end right there. JJ understood that Pa wasn't kidding. Pa had a no-tolerance attitude with some things and this was one of them. It was for the safety of the family and to provide a safe haven for deer that liked to come around the house to be fed by Pa.

JJ nurtured these sites for prime hunting. He would come home from work and ride around to check on the feeders. He and John Anston, one of his coworkers, built blinds and set them up a hundred yards away from the feeders. They already had them in place so the deer wouldn't be spooked come deer season.

In the fall, JJ advertised the leases at five hundred dollars for each deer blind in the *Dallas Morning News* and in the Lufkin paper. He filled all the blinds and grossed ten thousand dollars. He moved all the cattle out of the hunting areas. Hunters harvested several big deer off our land. JJ thought it was a smashing success until Pa told him that if we did this every year, in a few years nothing would be left. We needed to manage the deer herd. That meant fewer hunters next year and restrictions on the size of deer. We could charge more money for the large bucks.

I was glad I had missed the whole deer-hunting season. I was not sure my psyche could have handled the macabre sight of dead deer—animals I found so beautiful—hanging in trees in the hunting camps and the gruesome buckets of entrails being hauled off. The very thought made me tremble inside.

Pa didn't want hunters leaving piles of entrails lying all over the property, and some hunters actually didn't know how to field dress a deer. So, disposing of the entrails became a mammoth job. JJ bought several galvanized wash buckets for the hunters to place the guts in after the evisceration. JJ had taken the tractor into the lower lands and, about a hundred yards from the creek, dug a trench to dump the entrails into and eventually bury them.

Before he buried the gore, he had a pit full of nasty decaying stomachs, spleens, hearts, and miles of intestines. The turkey vultures caught on to the sight and had a feast. JJ finally buried it all under eighteen inches of dirt.

Chapter Four

JJ noticed after the hunt was over, and he had time to re-consider his strategy, that it was important to find out what size bucks we still had in this area. He started taking me out with him to observe. He knew I would never put another rifle in my hands, but I didn't mind observing the beautiful creatures. We spent hours sitting in blinds, arguing the merits of hunting and how unsportsmanlike it was to sit in a blind and shoot deer that have been trained to come feed at the same time each day. To me, it was like shooting fish in a barrel. JJ would argue how important it was to control the herd. The arguments never convinced either one of us. On the other hand, we also had many good laughs reflecting on our childhood.

As we drove around and checked the feeders, evidence of other animals was becoming more common. We saw wild turkey tracks, raccoon tracks, and hog tracks. The hogs were the most disturbing because they would wipe out the food supply before the deer could get to it. If there was an animal that could be the devil's own, it was a hog as far as we were concerned. Hogs made the feeders less attractive to the deer. Hog scat was everywhere, which also scared off much of the other wildlife.

"I heard there's good money in hog huntin'," said JJ as we sat in a blind one day and watched the hogs come in. There were twelve in this little herd: a young boar and an older boar keeping their distance, two sows, and eight young ones. "I think we need to open the property to hog huntin," JJ continued. "We could make money year 'round. People like the excitement of hog huntin'."

I wasn't keen on the idea of allowing hunting on our

property all year; although, as far as I was concerned, he could kill every hog. Looking at things now from an adult's perspective, I agreed, "They're going to hunt them somewhere else anyway."

"Why not bring the business here. There ain't no better place," said JJ.

I knew it would protect our pastureland by keeping it from getting rooted up and looking like a rototiller had gone through it. It would also take the burden off the feeders, and attract the deer back into this area.

JJ started doing his research. He wanted to know everything he could find out about hunting hogs. He found that Russian boars attracted hunters more than regular feral hogs. There was just something more exotic about them. Of course, most of the hogs were hybrids.

He discovered that they would come out in the day or night depending on the season and availability of food. What caught his eye the most was when he read that wild hogs were among the most intelligent animals. They knew their territory and could outsmart hunters and dogs by running to the thickest thickets, cattail patches, and briar patches. They were quick on their feet too.

Hogs could breed two litters a year and have four to six piglets each time. Also, they could breed at six months. These were prolific animals with few predators. Coyotes and bobcats would feed on their babies, but once hogs were adults, they had no natural predators. Nothing got in their way. They could eat almost anything; they were known as opportunistic omnivores. This means they could change their diet dramatically to adapt to the circumstances. They could not live too far from water and enjoyed wallowing in mud holes.

Contrary to deer, hogs would cover a wider range and would pick up and leave an area if something scared them. In addition to the scat and tracks at the feeders, Pa pointed out to us that the hogs were rooting in his prime pastureland, tearing up the grass and dirt looking for grubs and insects. One time, Pa buried a calf that died just after birth. Two days later, something dug it up and ate the whole thing. Pa was surprised because it was buried under a good foot of dirt. Hogs have a keen sense of smell and they found it, dug it up, and feasted on the rotting carcass.

JJ made another discovery too. He had been out managing his feeders in the spring and came back rather disturbed.

"You look like somebody stole your lunch money, JJ," Ma said coming up and gently hugging him. Ever since we were little, Ma always related our puzzled looks to having our lunch money stolen.

"I'm fine, Ma. It ain't nuthin'," he said to her and smiled. He sat at the kitchen table where I was enjoying my morning cup of coffee. He poured himself a cup and stared at it.

"What's eatin' you this mornin'?" I asked after Ma went to look after some laundry.

He looked down the hall to make sure Ma was out of hearing distance, then he told me soberly, "I drove by where I buried all them entrails and, before I saw anything, I smelled a horrific stench. I decided to find out what it was. I had to cover my mouth and nose before I lost my stomach, but I made my way toward the pit where I buried those guts. Just as I pulled over the hill to look down at the flat where I made the trench, I saw it was all dug up. And that giant hog we saw years ago, at least it looked like the one, was rollin' and wallerin' in those rotten guts along with thirteen other much smaller hogs. Billy, I swear it was that same big ol' hog. He's still around. As soon as they saw me, they scrambled outta there, except for him. He stood up and looked at me and his hair stood up along the ridge of his back. He shook his head and snorted like he was challengin' me or somethin'. I couldn't believe it, Billy. Those hogs dug up and feasted on those old entrails. From the looks of it, there musta been thirty hogs there last night." He never looked up from his coffee. "They're nasty beasts, Billy. I cain't believe they smelled out that pit under a good foot-and-a-half of dirt after this long. It was the horrid smell of death."

"Sounds purty nasty alright. I guess you need to go do a better job buryin' it," I said trying to lighten things up. I got no response for a moment.

Then JJ looked at me, "That big ol' razorback was sizin' me up and challengin' me. The hair along the ridge of his back was standin' straight up and a good four inches long. Just like a razor along his back. He looked at me like he was sayin' 'don't mess with me, buddy'."

"Oh come on, JJ. You been readin' too many of those hog books. They're smart, but they ain't that smart. You ain't tryin' to say that ol' hog remembers you, are ya?" I said laughing at him.

He looked at me intently, "You weren't there bein'

stared down by those cold, dark eyes, Billy. It's like he remembered me and was tryin' to tell me not to mess with
him," he said. He fell into a reflective trance.

"Come on, JJ. You been huntin' all your life. You know
animals don't think like that. It freaked me out too what we
had to witness as kids, but they just looked at Grant as easy
food at the time, that's all," I explained, trying to straighten
him out.

"Don't jack with me, Billy. I ain't crazy here. I know
what I saw." He was very focused on me now. "You remember years ago when Reverend Durham got his finger
bit off and we talked about whether animals got spirits? I
think I changed my mind. I saw one in that boar's eyes, a
devil spirit. I felt like I was starin' at Lucifer himself. I
think that hog deserves a name like Ol' Lucifer. I've been
thinkin' 'bout it anyway. Not too long ago, I was talkin' to
Reverend Durham. He's decided it's as exciting huntin'
hogs as anything he's ever hunted. He's the one that got me
thinkin'. He told me that when he got his finger bit off was
the first time he's been that close to a wild animal in total
terror of what's happenin' to it. Usually they're shot and
either dead or almost dead. When he was hog tyin' that
boar, he felt like it had a soul. He saw the terror in its
eyes."

"That's interesting. And he still likes to hunt?" I asked.

JJ gave me his let's-not-get-into-that-again look.

"Yes, Billy, he still likes to hunt! Now though, he pre-
fers to catch 'em alive and haul 'em off for money. He and
Sam are into it. In fact, they wanna come on our property. I
told 'em I'd let 'em for a couple hunts if they'd show me

the technique to dog huntin' for boars."

I just listened. I wasn't going to commit myself to anything.

"I'll get my rifle out and hunt Ol' Lucifer. Then we'll see how challengin' the boar wants to be when he's a pile of sausage links and bacon," he said changing thoughts again and with a little snarl.

Just then Ma walked back into the kitchen. "You boys are big enough to be out helpin' your pa. Days a burnin' and he let you sleep in, Billy. I know you been out already, JJ, but your pa could sure use both a your help to dust and vaccinate all those cattle. Y'all have other jobs I know, but this is still Pa's and my lifeblood."

We got the hint and scattered. Within a half an hour we were saddled up and helping Pa herd the cattle to the corral so we could run them through the chute and dust and vaccinate them. Pa didn't complain; he was just happy to see both of his boys out helping him. Pa was that way. He was an independent sort. Ever since we were about fourteen, if we didn't want to help, he just did it all himself and made us feel guilty watching him out breaking his back to take care of us. Ma was the one who filled in the blanks and put the Christian fear in us that if we didn't get out there and help, she'd see to it we didn't eat that night. She wasn't just talking either. I did go without a few meals when I thought I'd test her. As for Pa, he just gladly accepted our help when we were there.

Even though I'd get lazy sometimes, it was a pleasure to work alongside Pa. He was full of great stories and lessons on life. He would always relate life to things we did on the ranch. He was a wise man. Looking at him now, I realized why he was so to himself and didn't like being in crowds like church socials and just church. War has a way of doing that to a person. I love him even more having had that experience myself. I now work in a big city and ride mass transit to get to and from work, but I look around at all the people and feel like I'm looking through a glass cage at them. I can spot the ones that are a lot like me though. I see how they react around people getting too close. I just leave them alone too. That's what I prefer they do to me.

Working with Pa that day, JJ laid out his whole plan for developing hog hunting on the ranch. Pa patiently listened. He agreed there was just getting to be too big of a population around and they were starting to do too much damage. So, he decided to let JJ give it a try, declaring the same stipulations for staying well away from the house. He emphasized that this was a big ranch and some areas he hardly ever used, so there was no reason that he had to see hunters or hear the noise around the house scaring the horses. Excitedly, JJ agreed. Again, I stayed uncommitted.

Chapter Five

At church, with hog hunting on his mind, JJ invited Sam Kinkade to come over and show him what hog hunting was all about. Sam explained that he didn't shoot the hogs; he tried to take them back alive to sell to an export company. He agreed to come over early on Saturday morning and bring his horses and dogs. JJ was like a little kid waiting for Christmas, anticipating the Saturday hunt. He was excited for more reasons than just the hunt. He knew Sam usually brought his daughter along with him.

Saturday morning about three o'clock, the diesel pickup rumbled into the yard with the big, old horse trailer squeaking and rattling behind it and the dogs barking. The diesel idling stopped and the truck doors slammed. Then came the knock on the door. JJ had been awake since 2:30 a.m., anxiously awaiting this opportunity. From my bedroom, I could hear them talking and drinking coffee before unloading the horses and dogs.

"Where's Billy? I thought he'd enjoy this too," I heard Sam say.

"Aw, he's not into this kind of stuff, and ever since Vietnam, he's even more against it. I just don't bother him about it," said JJ in a respectful manner. I appreciated that.

"Well, Annie will be disappointed. She kind of likes him and was hopin' he'd be comin' along," said Sam.

I could feel the silence as JJ absorbed this. I knew he had a crush on Annie since we were kids. There hadn't been anything between Annie and me for years. I wanted to get up and say, "No, no, JJ, I don't have any interest in Annie." I knew she liked me ever since we were in high school. She was a year behind me. I just never cared to date a girl who could ride and rope circles around me and was nearly as tall as I was. She was gorgeous. That wasn't the problem. She had sandy brown hair nearly to her waist. She kept it in a braid most of the time. She didn't wear much makeup and had a beautiful complexion with just a few tiny freckles. Her eyes were the deepest green I'd ever seen and her smile was bright and well used. She fit into a pair of jeans like no other and was confident in herself. None of that was a problem. I just thought of her as the little sister I never had because she was just under me in age and we spent most of our lives in church and school teasing and making smart remarks to each other.

Anyway, I knew JJ had a crush on her and I knew if they spent time together, she'd probably find him more compatible to her style.

"S-so, where is she?" JJ stuttered.

"Oh, she's letting the horses out of the trailer and getting them ready."

"Does she need some help?" JJ asked.

"No, she's pretty good at it. But, if you feel the need, go ahead. Be my guest." Sam winked at him.

As JJ was leaving, Reverend Durham wandered in. "Mornin', JJ. God's given us another beautiful day and it's gonna be an exciting one too," he chirped. He was much too excited and jovial for this time in the morning. He had been out taking care of the horse he had purchased a few weeks ago. This was the first hunt for him with this new horse. He had no idea how this horse would respond to this kind of activity. If horses aren't used to dogs barking and wild boars snorting and squealing, they can get pretty spooked and become dangerous themselves.

"Mornin' to you, Reverend. You're serious about this, getting a new horse and all," responded JJ.

"This kinda stuff is the thrill of my life and it's great being around such great guys."

I thought that sounded a little patronizing. JJ didn't respond. I just heard the door shut.

I got up to see what was going on and saw JJ outside talking to Annie about the dog she had on a leash. Sam was getting the other dogs ready. They looked like bay hounds. They were just a bunch of mongrel hounds, but they knew what they were there for and were barking and getting excited to be released and get to business. The dog Annie held looked like a large pit bull. JJ already had Winnie May saddled up and had his 30-30 rifle in its saddle holster. They all got on their horses and headed out. The dogs were on long leashes so they could release them when they were ready. I jumped back in bed.

About midday, I was in the barn helping Pa repair a main door, rehanging it with new hinges, when Sam rode up for the truck. He unhitched the trailer and asked if he could put his horse in the corral. We agreed.

"How's the hunt goin', Sam?" I asked.

"It's goin' great. The boar swam across Longbow Creek and the dogs have him bayed on the other side. I figured it would be easier if I brought the truck down that other side instead of draggin' a hog across the creek." He then took off in a big hurry.

I didn't see anyone again until a couple hours later. The truck pulled in about the same time as the rest came back on their horses, dogs and all. I noticed JJ and Annie talking up a storm. I think I was the last thing on either of their minds. I could hear them laughing and carrying on about something.

When Sam pulled up in the truck, he had a hog tied up in the back still fighting and snorting. His snout was tied too, so he couldn't do any harm. He looked to be at least two hundred pounds. I think he was a hybrid. He still had a curly tail and Russians have straight tails. He was heavier built through the rump too. He would make someone a good ham hog.

I couldn't help but notice the wild-eyed look of terror in his eyes and his rapid breathing. He had evacuated his bowels all over the back of the truck and it stunk horribly. Although this animal couldn't think or reason like a human, I imagined that if he could break loose he'd slash anything he could with those three-inch tusks until he had cleared himself of this threat to his life. He would not look back and would have no thought of revenge, just safety…or would he think about it? I didn't think animals could think like that, but after looking at him, I wasn't so sure.

"He's a good one, ain't he?" Sam said as he walked up and leaned over the truck with me. "Annie hog tied him all by herself," he added, as though he had bragging rights.

"So whatta you do with him now?" I asked.

"He's fixin' to go to Indonesia. The processor I send 'em to exports the pork there," Sam explained.

When they all rode up, JJ jumped down, came over, and slapped me on the back. "Ain't he a beaut'? You shoulda seen Annie in action. She's fearless," he said. He looked at her and saluted. She smiled and saluted back. Goofy, but I guess it worked for them.

"I'm gonna have to tell y'all about it tonight. I want Pa to hear too," said JJ all excited.

"First time out and JJ handled things real well," reported Reverend Durham. He looked worn out.

"How did your horse handle things?" I asked innocently. I noticed everyone looking at me like maybe I had better leave it alone.

"No, everyone, that's a fair question. He didn't mean anything by it," he responded seeing the others' reaction. "This horse accepts riders real well and I thought things were gonna be easy. Little did I know what things were fixin' to happen. As soon as he heard the dogs change their tone to the high pitch when they're on to somethin', this horse decided it was time to hightail it back to the barn. I fought him until he reared and dumped me on my rear. Actually, I did a complete back flip off his rump."

Everyone got a good laugh out of that.

After the laughter settled down, Sam started barking orders to get everything packed up before they ran out of daylight.

We waved everyone off and went in the house. JJ stayed out a little longer to watch the truck drive off. Annie was turned around waving the whole way out. Something definitely happened out there that ignited their flames.

Pa didn't come in until almost nine o'clock. He sat at the table and we were all there already. He got himself some of Ma's casserole that was still sitting on the counter. He sat down to eat, then suddenly stopped, looked up, and realized everyone was staring at him.

"What the blazes are y'all lookin' at? I'm the one that works up the biggest appetite around here," he stated looking a little flustered.

JJ spoke up, "Don't you wanna know how the hunt went?"

Pa looked around at everyone again, then laid his fork down and sat back. "Well, I guess I do. Excuse my manners for not askin'. It's not like I'm starvin' or nuthin'. I haven't eaten since five this mornin'," he said sarcastically.

JJ just ignored the sarcasm and started in:

We took off on the horses this mornin' and couldn't see a thing; it was so dark. Winnie May knew the way and led the rest of the horses to the edge of the woods. That's where Sam let the dogs go. We just waited and listened as they made their way into the woods. You could tell as soon as they caught trail 'cuz their barkin' changed. Then, Sam told us to start movin' in slowly. Dawn was breakin' and we could see a little.

Sam told Annie to lead the way. She hadn't said much yet and I thought she was mad 'cuz Billy wasn't there. Turns out, she just don't talk unless she's interested in talkin'.

Anyway, she took the lead and ever so often she'd stop and put her hand up to silence us so she could listen to the dogs. We musta gone on like that for an hour or more. The dogs were gettin' quieter, so we decided we better trot the horses and catch up with 'em. We got to where the dogs were closer and kept listenin'. By now I was getting real anxious to see what was gonna happen next.

We followed the dogs until about eight thirty when the fever of their barkin' picked up. We knew they'd found somethin'. Annie looked back at us with an excited look and said, "Come on. They're on to somethin'. They got a hog!" I got all excited too, tryin' to anticipate what was gonna happen. We trotted our horses through the woods, tryin' not to get knocked off by low tree limbs. I have to say, I couldn't keep my eyes off Annie. I mean to tell ya, she looked good from behind on that horse.

We all laughed. JJ wasn't shy about the fact he'd fallen head over heels for this girl. I still felt bad about what Sam said to him this morning. But, obviously he had gotten over that. JJ continued:

We came to a tight briar thicket. We couldn't see nuthin', but the dogs were crazy and tryin' to find a way in. Annie had that big ol' pit bull, named Thor, up in the saddle with her. She wasn't ready to un-leash him yet.

We got off our horses to see what was in there. In that instant the reverend's horse went berserk on him. That horse was buckin' and rarin' until it rared high enough to dump the reverend off. He did a complete back flip and landed on his feet, then fell back on his butt. The reverend sat there dumb-founded and his horse was gone. Sam went chasin' it, caught it, and brought it back. It was embar-rassin' 'cuz we didn't know whether to laugh or show respect. We kept quiet until he started laughin' at himself. We all laughed along with him.

Just as Sam came back with the horse, and Annie and I were on the ground lookin' to get a better view of the hog, we spotted it. It was a beaut'. Thor wanted at the boar so bad, he was up on two legs pullin' at his leash. He was about to drag Annie through the briars, so she unleashed him. He charged the thicket and we heard a lotta squealin' and fevered barkin'. The noise was deafening. I never knew dogs and hogs could make that much noise. We heard Thor yelp a couple times. Annie got worried the boar might have slashed him. She yelled at me that they paid a thousand bucks for that dog. He was supposed to be the best hog dog on the market.

Suddenly, chargin' outta the thicket come this boar straight at me. I didn't have time to do nothin' but fall down. I'm just glad that boar didn't want a piece of me. He just wanted to get to the creek. Shakin', I got up and followed Annie, runnin' full speed, down to the creek.

The dogs had him bayed in a thick cattail patch. Thor ran in straight after it. We started in, and I was freaked out. I could hear the noise, but I couldn't see six inches in front of me. I just knew I was gonna part those cattails and find myself standin' nose to nose with an angry boar. But, I couldn't stop and let Annie show me up.

There was a lotta splashin', then Sam shouted that he just saw the boar swim across and Thor was on his tail.

"Y'all find a way to cross over. I'm goin' back for the truck and I'll meet ya'll on the other side," shouted Sam. Sam hightailed it in a big hurry.

Once he was gone, Reverend Durham suggested we let this hog go and try for another one that wouldn't be so hard to get back. Annie just looked at him impatiently and said, "Pa would whip the tar outta me if he thought I let this hog go after the dogs worked this hard."

We just looked around and luckily found a large downed sycamore tree that straddled the creek. I ran to it and started across. Annie and the reverend were right behind me. I stopped dead in my tracks. In front of me were four water moccasins hangin' in the tree.

"Come on!" shouted Annie.

"There's four water moccasins right in front of me and they're the biggest and fattest snakes I ever saw," I said backin' up.

Annie just said, "Get outta the way."

I obliged her and she started across jumpin' and shakin' the tree. The snakes didn't like it and dropped into the water. She went across no problem. I was impressed.

The reverend and I crossed and just watched as Annie and Thor worked their magic.

Thor was bleedin' from a couple spots on his leg and shoulder, but he had that boar solid by the ear. That boar squealed at an ear piercin' level, but it didn't move. Annie threw a rope around his rear legs and pulled as hard as she could. With his rear legs pulled tight together, he went down. Thor just kept pullin' on that ear. Carefully, Annie got the front two legs and had him hog tied: cinched up tight. Then she used a little rope and tied his mouth shut. She put the leash back on Thor and pulled him off. She praised him over and over.

It was an impressive sight, I tell ya. I ran up and high-fived her, then gave her a big hug and swung her around. I think she kinda liked it 'cuz she hugged me back and didn't let go. I told her how impressed I was, and she just smiled and stared into my eyes for a while. I couldn't take my eyes off of her. Then Sam came pullin' up, honkin' the horn.

It took all four of us to load that wigglin' hog, but we did. We gathered the dogs and headed back here. It was a great day. I cain't wait to do it again!

Chapter Six

Winter was completely gone and spring had arrived in full bloom. The days were warm, but still cooled off nicely in the evenings. East Texas becomes very popular in the spring. People from all over love to come here to see the wildflowers in bloom. Miles of Texas bluebonnets interlaced with Indian paintbrush, pink and yellow primrose, beautiful deep reddish-purple winecups, and brilliant yellow daffodils line the highways. As you look into the woods everywhere, interlaced among the bright-green new foliage of a wide variety of deciduous trees, are the large, almost-glowing white blossoms of the dogwoods and the lilac-colored blossoms of the redbud trees. It creates a visual feast and an excitement for the renewal of life in its abundance. Along with spring's abundance of life this particular year, were the blossoming relationships of JJ and Annie and my own relationship with a girl named Suzanne, whom I knew from high school.

Between JJ's occupation as a lineman and his preoccupation with Annie, I hardly saw him anymore. Thank goodness for Sundays; JJ would bring Annie over to spend some time with us. We got to hear about Annie's barrel racing competitions and how JJ was learning to rope alongside Sam. As long as JJ could rope, Sam couldn't find a thing wrong with him. Sam was trying to convince JJ that he'd be a good steer wrestler also. JJ didn't seem to be taking that one too seriously.

All I know is that JJ's life changed dramatically after he met Annie. Mine changed too. One Thursday afternoon, Pa asked me to run into town and pick up some supplies at the Lufkin Farm Implement Store. I knew where it was, but hadn't been there for years.

As I drove the farm-to-market road into town, I slowed down going by the McNeil place next to us. It was the residence of the Angelina County judge, Honorable Kenneth McNeil. Several police cars and people had gathered in the back pasture.

I got to the farm implement store and went straight in looking for what I needed. I wasn't much for shopping around and I usually tried to maintain a low profile so I didn't have to talk with anyone. I really didn't want a reoccurrence of the Bobby Hayden experience. I did notice, though, an exceptionally gorgeous young lady walking toward the checkout counter and talking with an old man who was going to buy a handful of items. It took me a minute, but I recognized her as Suzanne Wesley. She had been a lead cheerleader in high school and had never said one word to me. Silly as it was, I felt that high school intimidation well up in me again as I thought about the very idea of talking to her. I watched her as she helped the old man at the checkout stand and continued to talk and smile the whole time. She was blessed with feminine curves and her shoulder-blade length dark brown hair glistened silky and smooth. Every so often, almost subconsciously, she tucked one side of her hair behind her ear, revealing a set of silver loop earrings. She fit well into her tight-fitting jeans too. She was wearing the standard Lufkin Farm and Implement dark purple T-shirt. I was awestruck. I was determined to talk to her before I left the store.

The farm implement store was a place where old farmers would congregate and discuss town events if they didn't see each other at the twenty-four-hour diner. One of the conversations I overheard caught my attention. I situated myself to where I could listen in.

"Did ya hear what happened down on Judge McNeil's place?" asked one of the old men. It caught my attention because I had just gone by there.

"No," the other replied.

"Seems Judge McNeil's youngest son, Randy, was out behind the place with his cousin, Johnny McNeil, the judge's nephew. They were out explorin' the creek bottom with their BB guns, just givin' birds a run for their money. Accordin' to Johnny, they saw lizards and were havin' a great time tryin' to catch 'em. Johnny was chasin' his own lizard when Randy went down the creek bottom a little further around a bend…"

"Can I help you?" came a voice from behind me and made me jump. I turned around ready to hit someone, and saw Suzanne standing there startled and looking at me with those Bo Derek deep-blue eyes.

"Don't ever startle me like that. I got Vietnam syndrome!" I snapped at her. She backed off, feigning indifference.

"No, no, no. I'm sorry. I didn't mean that in a negative way. It's just somethin' I'm workin' on to get over," I said trying not to let her go and to make conversation.

"Hey, you're Billy Longbow. I read about you coming home a hero from Vietnam several months ago. That was quite a story about you. When I read it, I remember wondering why I never got to know you better. Weren't you on the football team?" she asked like nothing ever happened.

"Yeah, that was me. I never really made anything of myself playin' football."

"So what. What I remember was in our social studies class our senior year, the discussion, or should I say argument, you got into with a couple of the guys who were bragging about their great white hunter deer stories. I remember the teacher just let you guys go at it. Afterward, he explained that he allowed it because it was a good topic that everybody seemed interested in, y'all were keeping it reasonably civilized, and were using some good information and reasoning. I remember thinking how much more of a stud you seemed to me because you didn't have to prove your manhood by killing innocent animals. And, I remember how stupid you made the other guys sound. I remember wondering why you hadn't ever asked me out since everyone else on the football team had."

I couldn't believe what was happening. Here was a girl I

considered out of my league telling me she wanted to go out with me—at least years ago she wanted to.

"I always thought you and Andy Jones were a thing, so I never thought about it," I explained.

"We were for a while, but when I wanted to break it off, he wouldn't stay away and he'd hover over me like no one better even think of dating me. He went to Vietnam too. He was killed in the Tet Offensive."

"Oh, I'm sorry to hear that. That was one of the worst situations over there."

"I felt bad when I heard it, but I also felt released," she added.

"Hey, I don't mean to cut you off, but did you hear 'bout what happened at the McNeil place?" I asked her, trying to be as polite as I could.

"No. I've noticed a lot of scuttlebutt going on, but I usually don't pay much mind to it," she responded.

"Come with me before that old guy leaves. I need to know what he knows 'cuz it's right next to our place." We walked over to where the two elderly gentlemen were talking.

"Excuse me. I couldn't help overhearin' ya. I'm Billy Longbow and we live next to the McNeil place."

The old guy looked at me rather shocked. "Ya better be careful 'cuz there's a madman butcher loose out there. He cut up Judge McNeil's boy."

Suzanne drew back in shock, covering her mouth. "Randy? It can't be. I used to babysit him. He's a good kid." She was visibly shaken. "I got to go. I can't take this." She hurried off, but then stopped. "Billy, call me tonight, please, and tell me what you find out."

I turned back to the old man and asked him how he knew all this and what else he knew.

"My wife's the sheriff's dispatcher. She knows every-thin' 'round here," the old man proclaimed, looking insulted that I questioned him. I didn't care. I needed to know how true it was.

"Tell me what happened after the kid went around the bend," I asked trying to be more polite.

"Ya know this boy was only eleven, don't ya?"

"Yeah, yeah, go on," I said.

The old man continued:

Well, Johnny, the judge's nephew, said Randy disappeared 'round the bend and then a few minutes later, Johnny heard Randy screamin' and screamin' loud. Then, he said he heard somethin' like some snortin' and snarlin' and at the same time Randy was makin' sounds while he was screamin' like he was bein' thrown around and squished. Then it all went quiet.

Johnny said he was so scared he just hid under a bush, shakin' for a long time. He said he was thinkin' he was next. Finally, when he thought it was all clear, he came out. He slowly sneaked around the bend—still afraid to make any sounds. He peeked around and could just barely see part of Randy. He said he slowly walked to him and didn't see nuthin' at first. But, when he got closer, he saw

a pool of blood 'round his head and innards everywhere.

When he got to him, he found him layin' there
with a deep gash across his neck and up his face.
The boy said Randy was layin' funny and his abdomen was slashed open with his innards pulled out
all over the ground. The area was soaked in blood.

Mrs. McNeil said she heard Johnny screamin'
the whole way back to the house. She came runnin'
out to meet him and see what was wrong. She said
Johnny was hysterical and shakin' so bad he
couldn't talk. She sensed somethin' bad happened
to Randy and she yelled at Johnny to tell her where
Randy was. All he would do was shake his head and
cry hysterically. She told him to go to the house and
she went after Randy. She followed Johnny's tracks
through the grass back to the creek.

Johnny said he saw her screamin' an' runnin'
back with her hands flailin' in the air. He called
9-1-1. When the sheriff's deputy and the ambulance
got there, Mrs. McNeil led 'em back there and the
sheriff commented that it looked like somethin' had
eaten most of his intestines and soft organs. It was
indeed a gruesome sight. What coulda done somethin' that terrible? I know Judge McNeil just got
done sentencin' that guy who stole his girlfriend's
kids; beat the boy an' left him for dead at the city
park an' took the girl an' raped her then slit her
throat. Maybe it was one of his relatives tryin' to
get revenge. That's what they're sayin', but I think

it was some animal.

The old guy told me much more than I wanted to know. I had to pass the McNeil place on the way home. Later that evening, I related the whole story to my family. JJ even stopped long enough to listen.

I downplayed the boy's story because I wanted to tell my parents about Suzanne. They remembered her well and encouraged me to call her. Before I did though, Ma warned me in a quiet way that Suzanne's mother had passed away a couple years ago. Her father had become a fall-down drunkard and had his driver's license taken away when he got in a wreck with a young girl, who was seriously injured. The family had sued him for all he was worth. Now he had nothing and he was known to be cruel to Suzanne.

I weighed this all out and decided to call her anyway. I was fortunate; I caught her when her father was gone—drinking. I shared the rest of the story with her in a toned-down version. I could tell she needed company. So, I asked if she wanted to go out and see a movie or something. She happily agreed. It was the start of a wonderful relationship.

Chapter Seven

I got dressed in my best jeans and boots and put on a spiffy new shirt with pearl snap buttons. I was ready to dazzle Suzanne. She had given me her address, but in the process of talking about the McNeil incident, I forgot to ask her for directions. I looked it up in the phone book. I thought I had something wrong, because it was in the low-income, black side of town. She told me she'd leave the porch light on so I'd know I had the right place.

I drove through town and over the tracks. Lufkin definitely had an "other side of the tracks" section. You knew it was fixing to get bad if you had to go over there, so I hadn't spent much time in that part of town. It took some driving around to figure things out, but I found the house on time. It was a humble, little, old, asbestos-siding house painted white with a small single-step front porch. The yellow bug light on the front porch was on. Eleven-seventy-eight North Orchard—that had to be the place. The yard was small, but—contrary to the surrounding cluttered, dirty yards and old frame houses covered with green moss from the humidity—it was clean, and the grass was green and bright. There were actually flowers in the yard.

Nervously, I walked up and knocked on the screen door. The inside door was open and I could hear country music on the radio. Don Williams was singing one of his easygoing songs. I waited a few seconds then knocked again.

"Just a second," I heard from the back room.

As I waited, I looked through the rusty screen at the living room. It was small and packed full of furniture all focused toward the TV, the standard American living room. It smelled old but clean. Then I saw a profile coming from the kitchen into the living room. It was Suzanne.

"Hi Billy, come on in," she casually said. I hesitantly made my way in. It was now getting into the heat of the late spring and I noticed that, except for the breeze, it was awfully warm in the house. "Forgive me, I am just trying to find my shoes. I have a bad habit of taking them off in different places just to get them off my feet as quick as I can."

I just smiled and patiently waited. I looked around the living room at the pictures on the table and on the walls. There were pictures of Suzanne as I remembered her, in her cheerleading suit, caught in midair doing a cheer. Suddenly the intimidation welled up inside me again and I had to remind myself that we were adults now and a lot of water had gone under the bridge.

She came out ready to go. She looked stunningly beautiful in her soft, pink-pastel, sleeveless blouse that accented her bright-blue eyes, her well-fitted, khaki-colored slacks and, when she finally found them, her white sandals. I could tell she had just run a brush through her silky brown hair. She just let it fall free on her shoulders.

She walked up to me, put both hands on her hips and smiled, "You look good, cowboy," then walked by me, ready to go.

I shook my head, cracked a smile, and opened the screen door for her. She walked past me onto the porch. I caught a smell of her sweet perfume on the way out.

"Do you need to shut the door?" I asked.

Casually, she looked over her shoulder. "No, we don't have any air conditioning so it gets sweltering in there if the door is closed and, that way, Dad can find his way in."

Her last comment puzzled me, but I didn't say anything. I gently rested my hand on the small of her back and led her to the pickup. I opened the door for her. She glanced my way, smiling, and swung her hair to one side as she got in. As I shut the door, I could feel my heart racing; she was knock-dead gorgeous.

We drove in uncomfortable silence for a while on our way to the movie theater. She turned to me before we got there, "What do you say, instead of going to a movie, we go somewhere we can get caught up on our lives for the past few years?"

"Sure, you got anywhere in mind?" I asked eagerly.

"I haven't been dancing for well over a year. Are you up for it?" she asked, looking at me with a sly expression, offering me a subtle challenge.

"Yeah, I used to be a purty good dancer, but it's been a few years with Vietnam in between," I said trying to provide an excuse if I stepped on her foot. I was also a little self-conscious of my limp.

"Ah, you'll catch on just like riding a horse. And I'll bet a cowboy like you knows how to swing a girl around pretty good." She looked at me and winked. I took it all in jest.

We decided to go to the Trail's End Bar. The place was hopping with people starting their weekend, and a local country band was playing some good boot-scootin' country music. We found a table and no sooner sat down and a couple of her girlfriends spotted us. They came over with their boyfriends and introduced themselves. The girls immediately sat down and started talking and laughing with Suzanne and throwing questions at me. It didn't take long for the subject of Vietnam to come up. The girls all remembered me from high school. They looked familiar, but weren't folks I used to hang out with. I knew the guys too. One was quite friendly, but the other two looked like they'd rather be somewhere else. At that moment, I was getting all the attention and they didn't like it.

One of them made the comment, "What's the big deal about Vietnam? Anyone can shoot a gook."

I could tell he was arrogant and needed a little humbling. I figured I was just the man to do it.

I focused my gaze on him, "I don't recall askin' for your opinion. You were probably too scared to go. What'd you do, hide behind your momma's apron strings? Join some bleeding heart society? I was there and took a bullet in my thigh and watched all my patrol buddies—excellent quality men, I might add—get slaughtered so you could stay home and drink beer and do nothin' with your puny life but chase skirts."

The guy puffed up his chest trying to size me up. I stood up and my chair flew back. I walked over to him and stood toe to toe.

I said quietly in his face, "Buddy, I ain't into idle threats." I stared at him waiting for the message to sink in and waiting to see if he would act. He squirmed and turned away from my gaze. "Good decision, buddy. The next good decision is ta act like an adult, grow up, and quit tryin' to show off by pickin' fights."

I cracked a smile at him to ease the tension, and patted him on his upper arm, turned around and politely asked Suzanne if she would like to dance. I had to get away from the crowd. She looked at me with a dazed and shocked look in her eyes, but got over it quick, "Yes, cowboy, I'd love to dance."

It was a slow one and I pulled her in tight. "Do you find yourself having to do that often?" she asked in an unoffensive way.

"More than I like. I don't get a kick out of it, but I won't back down to the honor of servin' my country."

"I heard about your confrontation at the convenience store with Bobby Hayden. I didn't think much of it when I overheard the lady talking about it. It must have just happened. Then the lady came into the implement store talking about it. I remember thinking to myself, that wasn't the Billy Longbow I remembered." She paused for a moment looking right into my eyes. My goodness she was stunning. She made my heart stop for a moment, "You really saw your buddies get blown away in Vietnam?" she asked.

I tried to determine why she was asking this question and I knew I was the one that said something earlier. I decided she was sincere and if we were going to get to know each other, she might as well know up front what I was about.

"We were defendin' another patrol an' helpin' them get out of a hot spot with our chopper. I got shot and was flown out. When I came to, I asked 'bout my buddies and found out they were all slaughtered. It's taken me a long time to come back to bein' relatively normal. I carried so much anger and guilt for gettin' wounded and not bein' there for 'em. It wasn't too long ago, I woulda taken a guy like that's head off before I asked questions; so that was purty mild."

"That was Brandon Williams. As long as I've known him he has tried to intimidate people. I was proud of you. He needed to be put in his place."

We danced quietly for a few minutes.

"I read the article in the paper about you and kind of remember your story, but they left a lot of details out and now it means more because I know you," she said trying to talk over the music, but staying close to me.

We didn't talk any more for the moment. She just laid her head on my chest and enjoyed the music as we two-stepped around the dance floor. Neither one of us were drinkers, so I whispered in her ear, "Would you like to get out of here and go for a walk?"

"I love to go for walks," she responded all bright eyed.

We didn't even say good-bye to anyone. We just left the bar, jumped into the truck, and went to the Lufkin zoo and park where we could be alone and walk around the little lake. It was a steamy night. Between the cicadas, crickets, and tree frogs, the night was buzzing at almost a deafening level, but we didn't care. We walked and talked for hours about everything in our lives from high school on and laughed about our near-miss encounters in high school. As the night drew later, neither of us wanted it to end.

Through the night, I had skirted the subject of her father, but I still had a strong desire to know what had happened and how she was handling it.

"I know this is gettin' personal," I probed, "but what happened to your pa to turn him into an alcoholic? I was told it happened after your ma died."

"I don't mind. I'm not so afraid to talk about it anymore, and you should know anyway if we intend to see each other again." I just smiled to relieve the tension.

"Just after high school, I enrolled at Stephen F. Austin College and was looking forward to living on my own. We lived in a nice home just outside the highway loop on the southwest side of town. My mother was a very giving person and would do anything for me. My father, on the other hand, was a workaholic, and ever since I was about twelve, even living in Chicago before we transferred here, he seemed to be gone all the time. I went to live in the dorms with some of my girlfriends; a couple of them you met tonight. When I was gone, my mom and dad got in a fight. To this day, he has never told me what it was about. He backhanded my mom and knocked her down. She hit the kitchen table with the back of her head and was knocked cold. It scared him and he carried her to the bed. She regained consciousness and he cried for hitting her. She forgave him and everything was supposed to be okay. The next day, she had a major headache, took a couple of Excedrin, and went in to lie down. She never woke up again. The coroner said she had a massive aneurysm caused by a blow to the back of her head. The police investigated the death. My father told them she slipped on some water on the floor a couple nights before and he had carried her to her bed to lie down. They accepted it because there was no other proof. The problem, though, was that he knew what he had done and never to this day has forgiven himself. He thinks he can drown his guilt. He loved her in his own way with all his heart. I had to drop out of school to take care of him, because when he's drunk, he cries and grieves her loss and I know he'll drink himself to death. At least if I'm there, he feels like he's got something to come home to.

"He was coming home one night about this time last year and hit a young girl when he swayed into the other lane. He didn't hit her head on but grazed her enough to send her off the road into a tree. She's in rehabilitation, but she'll be okay. Her family sued us because Dad was drunk. They got everything and all we can afford on my salary is our little rental house," she said with disdain.

"Where does he get the money to go drinkin'?" I asked.

"He gets a Social Security check and has a little from what would have been his retirement money…and steals my money if I'm not careful," she said a little angrily.

"Do you ever worry about your safety?" I asked. "He does have a history a violence."

"I can take care of myself. I can be tough if I need to

be," she declared, looking at me with a smirk on her face.

"I want you to know, Suzanne, if you ever feel threatened, get out and call me. I'll come get you. You won't have to stay on the street."

"I appreciate that, you don't know how much. But, we really don't know each other that well. You may not even like me when you wake up tomorrow," she said looking away.

I gently held her chin and turned her head so I could look into her eyes, "I feel like I've known you forever. I know it's just been one night, but I've known you and had a crush on you for a long time."

We just looked into each other's eyes under the park light. I pulled her close and she wrapped her arms around my waist. I couldn't resist any more. I bent down and gave her a kiss. She responded by taking her arms from around my waist and putting them around my neck. She pulled me in tight and we stood there under that light kissing for a long time.

I knew it was getting late, so trying to be a gentleman, I told her I had better take her home. She looked at me, "No, let's just stay here and feel this forever."

It was tempting, but I just smiled at her and coaxed her along. Teasingly, she just rolled out of my grasp and whimpered, "No, I don't wanna go home. This is too nice."

I held her again and gave her another little kiss. "Come on, your dad will kill me for keepin' you out too late."

"My dad is probably too incoherent to realize I'm gone." She then jumped on my back and I carried her to the truck.

We drove to her home in relative silence. When we got

there, the lights were on, so I knew her dad was home. When I got out to open the door for her, I could hear her dad in the house ranting about something. I walked her to the door and there he was staggering in the living room.

"Are you sure you'll be okay?" I asked, getting a little concerned.

"I'll be alright. I've been through this many times before. I just get him ready for bed and see that he safely gets there."

"Hey, who are you?" It was her dad. He spotted me and staggered my way. "Hey, you datin' my daughter? She's a cutie, ain't she?" he slurred. He put his arm around her— more to hold himself up.

"Go, Billy, I promise I'm all right." She blew me a kiss.

"Yeah, come back and see us. You and I need to talk. You datin' my daughter, we need to talk," said her dad as she pulled him to the bedroom. I stayed on the porch and listened to make sure all was well, then left for home.

Chapter Eight

Spring and summer became a time for love around our house. I had made a regular thing of dating Suzanne, and we were getting along very well. I took advantage of every opportunity to go to the farm implement store. It seemed that whenever I stopped by, Suzanne introduced me to someone; some were old friends from high school and some were relatives. I had brought her out to the house to meet the family several times, and they all enjoyed her. She brightened things up every time she came. She and Annie hit it off immediately and almost had JJ and me nervous that they were going to enjoy each other more than us. When I would get that way, I would grab Suzanne, and we'd go horseback riding. I put her on Rounder, and I would take Winnie May.

We had a Fourth of July celebration at the house. We lit fireworks, and Pa fired up the smoker and smoked a couple briskets. Ma spent the day with the girls making potato salad, beans, and corn on the cob. Pa also had the ice cream maker going, making good old vanilla. He figured that way everyone could top it however they wanted.

Pa, who was usually quiet, opened up and became quite a joker when the girls were over. Maybe his personality would have been different if he would have had a daughter. Without saying anything, I think he thought of these two girls as potential daughters.

Pa's dream came true. I noticed JJ and Annie were secretive most of the evening. After the celebration ended and everyone was too full to move, JJ and Annie stood up to announce that they had become engaged, and they intended to get married next October. Ma screamed and clutched her heart then jumped up and hugged Annie. She completely ignored JJ, but you could tell he didn't care. He was a proud man. They took off soon after the announcement to tell Annie's family.

The party was breaking up, so Suzanne and I said our good-byes, and I drove her home. She nearly talked my ear off about how excited she was for JJ and Annie. She just thought they made the perfect couple, kind of like we did. Then she stopped herself and was embarrassed. She looked at me with her mouth open. I looked at her, winked, and laughed. I didn't say a thing, but I thought how right she was.

We drove to the house, and the lights were on. Suzanne's dad appeared in the doorway—holding a bottle of rum. I kissed Suzanne good night at the truck and sent her on her way.

"Where y'all been tonight? You don't think I'm good

enough to celebrate with?" her dad babbled. I watched Suzanne walk through the door.

She looked back at me then mouthed, "I'll be okay, go on!"

I was nervous leaving her with him in that mood. As I drove home, I couldn't think about anything except that I'd kill him if he ever hurt Suzanne. It eased my mind when I realized she had grown up with the guy; and she had never told me about any beatings, even though Ma said it had happened before.

I got home exhausted and walked into the house. Ma was on the phone and sounded distressed.

"What is it, Ma?" I asked, becoming concerned too.

She looked up at me. "It's Suzanne. She's at the gas station. She had to run away. Her dad was gettin' abusive. You better go get her before her dad figures out where she is."

I ran out of the house, jumped into the truck, and spun the tires getting out of the driveway. All I could think of was how I was going to kill him if he hurt Suzanne. I was lucky that night that there were no sheriff's deputies out to stop me. Although, I think they would have understood and probably escorted me to the station. When I got there, she was shaken up, crying, and reaching for me. She had a bruised and swollen lip, and her hair was matted where it looked like her dad had pulled on it. The top two buttons on her blouse were torn off, exposing her bra. That was the least of my concerns. I put her in the truck and headed for home.

"Are you okay? He didn't break anything did he? I'd

like to go beat him into oblivion myself," I rambled in a blind fury.

"I'm okay, nothing's broke. I don't know what happened. He kept rambling about being alone on the Fourth; that we were always together on the Fourth. I told him that I didn't want to sit at home and watch him drink until he blacked out. After that, when I wasn't looking, he came after me and started pulling my hair. When I turned around to grab his hands and make him let go, he decked me. I just got up and ran out of the house. I love him, but I wasn't going to stay around and have him do to me what he did to my mom. For the first time in my life, I am really, truly relieved." Her voice quivered.

I looked at her and she was crying like a baby. I pulled her close to me.

"You'll be okay now. Like I said, there's plenty of room at our house. You can stay with us until you get this worked out—or forever."

She looked at me and laughed between her crying. I hugged her tight.

"I wanna go over there and beat the fool out of him," I said again.

"Don't go after him, Billy. I don't want anything to happen to you, like ending up in jail. I'm okay now," she said as she snuggled up to me again.

"I won't. But I won't let anything happen to you either. I've lost too many loved ones in my life, and I'm not losin' you."

The house was dark as we drove past the McNeil home. "I wonder how they're doing after their tragedy. Have they figured anything out yet?" Suzanne asked.

"No, haven't heard a thing," I responded.

The next morning, everyone was looking at things from a different perspective. We all sat around the table. It was exciting having Suzanne there first thing in the morning. She was in one of Ma's robes, but she still looked cute. I teased her about how tough she looked with a fat lip. It had gone down quite a bit, but had turned even more purple.

JJ finally dragged up and had a big ol' smile on his face. He was feeling on top of the world. It made him feel even better to see Suzanne sitting there.

"So you decided to move in and just live with Billy I see. Okay Ma, if I thought you'd be that easy, why did I ask Annie to marry me? I shoulda just asked her to move in with us. I didn't think you'd go for it, but maybe I was wrong," he kidded.

Ma scowled at him. "Now, you know better than to even talk like that, JJ. We got us a guest for a while, and she's proper about it. Besides, knowin' Annie's pa, he'd be over here with a shotgun chasin' your hide around the yard tellin' you to hold still so he can take a good shot at you."

We all laughed at Ma, and Suzanne stood up and slapped JJ on the arm for saying it.

"What was that for?" asked JJ, acting innocent.

"That was for nothing. Just wait till you really do something," Suzanne quipped.

JJ sat down to his coffee and pancakes. "I heard the sheriff's deputies have been snoopin' over at the McNeils' and callin' it an investigation. Word has it, all they can find down there is a bunch of cow tracks, like they had been runnin' around in the creek bed too."

"Cow tracks?" I questioned. "They don't think a cow did it, do they?"

"I don't know how stupid they are. But, I have a theory, and I'm goin' to sneak over there today and take a look around too," said JJ.

"You can get in a lot of trouble tamperin' with evidence you know," I responded.

"I know that. Remember, I'm the hunter of the family. I'll be in there and out, and they won't never know I was there. My theory is that it was the work of that big ol' razorback we been seein'. His tracks are about as big as cow tracks an' I think the deputies don't know a cow track from a hog track. If it is hog tracks, we need to know it and do somethin' 'bout it," declared JJ.

Things got quiet and serious.

"Oh, stop talkin' that foolish stuff, JJ. Just because you and Billy saw something years ago doesn't mean that's what happened again," said Ma. She sounded worried. I sensed she actually thought that maybe JJ was right.

"I'm goin' over there today. Just don't break my cover."

After breakfast, I got ready to go meet Pa out in the field. He had been working all morning. I knew it was getting to be time for me to do something with my life, but Pa and Ma knew I'd take care of it and never said a word to me. I deeply appreciated that. I fully intended to go that fall and enroll in college and utilize my GI bill. I had talked about it with Suzanne; I just had no idea at the time what I wanted to study. For the summer, though, Pa was more than happy to have my services around the ranch.

Chapter Eight

We had to do something about clothes for Suzanne. She put her jeans on and I provided her with a T-shirt. She wanted to follow me around in the field and see what I did all day long. She was supposed to go to work, but she was afraid her dad would come looking for her. I told her that it was going to be hot out in the field and that she could stay and help Ma around the house. She didn't want any of that. She wanted to stay with me. I didn't mind.

We hopped in the truck and chased down Pa. He had a project going where a bunch of fence had been torn down. We found him—and just in time. He asked me to help him stretch some barbed wire, since it went a lot better with two people. He was pleased to see Suzanne and kindly greeted her. He was soaking wet with sweat, so I knew what I'd look like in just a little while.

"Those durn hogs have torn holes in the fence all over, and the cattle keep gettin' out onto the new grass. Those hogs are rootin' it up and destroyin' the field too. I just keep fixin' the fences. JJ needs to get more people in here and at least just scare 'em off to somewheres else," said Pa.

I jumped right in helping him. Suzanne sat on the truck tailgate watching us and asking questions like a little kid. She kept telling Pa and me how strong we looked and that we were the real cowboys; not the ones at the bars who wore suits all day then came decked out like cowboys on the weekends to dance. Pa was having fun listening to her and answering her questions. I just kept quiet and watched the relationship develop.

We'd put in a good day's work when JJ finally rode up on Winnie May.

"Oh, JJ, she's such a beautiful horse and she minds you well," said Suzanne.

"Hi. Yeah, I been ridin' her for about ten years now I guess. She purty much knows what I want. She's turned out to be a great ropin' horse now too," JJ responded.

"What did you find out?" I asked not being able to handle the suspense.

"It's just what I figured. I was in there and out before anyone knew I was there. Sure enough, it's hog. They're the biggest hog tracks I ever saw, but I know a hog track when I see one. I could see some spots in the softer mud where the dewclaws made prints. Cows don't leave dew claw prints."

"Wow, that's pretty good tracking, JJ," Suzanne commented.

JJ just pretended he didn't hear her; but knowing him like I did, I knew that bolstered his ego even more.

"So, what you gonna do now? Tell the sheriff that there's a man-eatin' hog runnin' loose?" Pa said. "These folks cain't comprehend that. The Honorable Judge McNeil will laugh you off his property. He's out to hang someone."

"I already did tell the sheriff, that's why I'm just gettin' here. I drove to the sheriff's office after I was over there and told him what I found. He looked at me like I was loony and wrote a note like it was a formality to do it while I was standin' there. Maybe he don't believe me, but it was my duty to set the record straight, and they'll know what I said if anyone else shows up dead," JJ announced.

"JJ, you gotta do somethin' 'bout this hog population around here," said Pa. "They're tearin' the fences down.

Chapter Eight

Fur a long time they just crawled under. Now they're tearin' 'em down. That's why I do believe you about big hogs. They're not far off because they're gettin' into the newly seeded fields every night on the edges and rootin' 'em all up and destroyin' the pasture. I'm tellin' you to get a huntin' party together and get a bunch of dogs out here."

I had never seen Pa so worked up before about animals.

"I gotcha, Pa. Consider it done," replied JJ. "I'll talk to Annie tonight and see about usin' her dogs. And I'll get Reverend Durham, my buddy John Anston, and see if Sam will help out again too. We'll put together a big huntin' party and run a bunch of 'em outta here before some other kid ends up dead."

Chapter Nine

JJ had big plans for the weekend. He was making a lot of noise about how he was going to put a hurt on the hog population. We knew our ranch was too big to clean house on the hogs entirely; and JJ did want some hogs left, in order to run his hunting guide business. This hog hunting was still new to him.

He had gotten the good reverend on board promising that they wouldn't run the hunt on Sunday. JJ took some vacation time to start on Thursday and run a three-day hunt. What he hadn't told anyone but me was his determination to find and hunt down the giant razorback. He swore he would do anything to bag that boar before it hurt or killed anyone else.

I remember asking him, "JJ, do you really know what you're gettin' yourself into, huntin' these vicious and smart animals without rifles?"

"Billy, for the first time in my life I feel like I'm hunting in a challengin' way. The odds still may be much more in our favor, but it does provide the animal a chance for a good fight. Besides, Sam showed me how we can make purty good money bringin' 'em back alive. Ol' Mr. Kramer up north of town takes as many live hogs as we can supply him and pays us $80.00 and up for any hog over a hundred and fifty pounds. He sells 'em to some exporting place that ships 'em off to Indonesia somewhere," he said, actually getting rather serious with me. "You know you can still come along if you want."

"No thanks, JJ. I love you as a brother and all, but Suzanne's still a whole lot cuter than you," I teased.

"Well, you gotta point there. I just don't see what she sees in your face that I thought only a mother could love," he said, pinching me on the cheek. We both laughed as he headed out the door to make the final arrangements he needed for the hunt in the morning.

Before he left, I asked him one more question. "JJ, if you run into that big razorback, do you really think those dogs can stand up to him? He ain't no ordinary boar, and he ain't lived this long bein' stupid."

JJ turned to face me. "That hog's goin' down," was all he said. Then he walked out the door.

I watched him leave and thought to myself, "That boy's got no fear. I'd be proud to have him by my side in any war."

The next day, the whole party was gone well before sunrise. I was drinking my morning coffee when Suzanne came into the kitchen. She wasn't used to this early morning rising. Pa had already gone out to feed the cattle, and

Chapter Nine

Ma had gone into town to run errands and do some volunteer work for the church.

"So why don't you hunt with your brother, especially when it's a big deal like this?" Suzanne asked, as she fiddled with her coffee. At first I was a little offended thinking that it shouldn't be hard to figure out, but I answered after some thought.

"To start with, I'm very different than my brother in that respect. I've never gotten pleasure outta killin' animals. Secondly, after Vietnam, I don't need anymore blood and guns."

She looked up at me with her elbows resting on the table and her hands folded under her chin. I could see the tenderness in her eyes. She slowly reached out and grasped my hand, then said, "That's what I love about you. Life is so deep and rich when I'm with you. You can be hard and fearless when you need to be and soft as a child other times." She smiled, leaned over, and kissed me.

After we finished our coffee she said she had a big favor to ask of me. "I'm really concerned about my dad. I'm not wanting to put myself in harm's way, but I am concerned. I called the implement store yesterday afternoon and told them I'd be back today. They want me at 9:00 a.m. Could you drop me off and then please..." and she paused, "please check on my dad."

"Sure, I can do that. Maybe I can convince him now that he needs to get help. Maybe you movin' out got his attention," I said, trying to be optimistic.

"Maybe so. I just worry that when we went back over there the other day to get my things, and he wasn't there, that he was on another binge. He's never gone during the day."

We left for town that morning, and I dropped Suzanne off at the implement store, ran my errands, then drove to her house. When I got there, the door was shut. It was just too hot of a morning to have that house closed up if he was home. I walked up to the porch assuming he wasn't home and just walked in.

"Mr. Wesley?" I yelled just in case he was home.

It didn't take long to figure out that something was wrong. The house had a sour odor as if someone hadn't taken the trash out when it had chicken parts sitting in it too long. The odor was not horrific yet, but bad enough to be repugnant.

The odor got worse as I got closer to Mr. Wesley's bedroom. I had a sickening feeling about what I would find. I looked in and there was Mr. Wesley lying on his bed in a wife-beater T-shirt—how ironic—and his boxers. He was definitely dead. There were two vodka fifth bottles—one on the floor and one lying beside him—both empty. Who knew how much he may have had before he ended up there. He was a grayish color and his eyes were dry and glazed open. The face muscles were totally relaxed and sagged. His arms and legs had straightened out and bloated. From the smell, it was obvious that the last thing he accomplished in this world was to urinate on himself. I was grossed out but not shocked. I had seen a lot of death in the past few years.

I have to admit that I regretted having to tell Suzanne, but personally I had no regrets seeing a wasted man like him gone. I had no respect for him.

I left quickly and drove around for a while trying to decide how and when to tell Suzanne. The guy could just stay there until someone else found him for all I cared. I knew we'd have to go through all these Christian formalities when all he needed was to be thrown in a cheap pine box and buried deep enough to quit stinking.

I decided I would be in trouble with Suzanne if I didn't tell her as soon as possible. I drove to the store, parked, and walked in. Suzanne was excited for a brief moment, but read the look on my face. She stopped right in the middle of checking out some cowboy's goods. She walked up to me staring me down the whole way.

"He's dead, isn't he?" was all she said.

I looked at her for a moment, then slowly shook my head, "uh huh." She turned around and saw the manager helping a customer. She politely interrupted him. He turned to face her and got a sorrowful look. The jerk used it as a chance to give her a long hug then told her to go. She rather coldly came back to me and said, "Let's go."

We got in the truck without a word being said and I pulled out, having no idea where we were going.

"Let's go back over there. I want to see for myself," she asserted.

"Are you sure that's a good idea? It ain't a pretty scene," I warned.

"I want to see him for myself," she said without expressing any emotion.

When we got there, I told her I wasn't going in again. She just marched right in. She was inside for about five minutes, then came out and wanted to leave.

"We need to do somethin'," I said to her.

"Like what?" she snapped.

"Like call the cops or somethin'. Come on, girl, he was your dad!"

She tried to act cold and uncaring at first. "Yeah, he was my dad. He was never there for me anymore. He killed the person that meant the world to me, left a path of destruction, and then ruined my life expecting me to take care of him every waking hour. Until I met you, Billy, I had no life. I feel like I've been freed from being his slave," she said venomously. Then tears filled her eyes. I stopped the truck and reached over to give her a hug.

When she regained her composure, I said, "Well, let's go tell the cops. They're gunna at least want a statement from us."

We drove to the Lufkin police station and had to hang around for a good hour before we were finally able to give a statement. They asked Suzanne where she wanted the body delivered. She told them she didn't care what they did with it; she didn't have any money for a funeral or casket. They told her they could give him a pauper's burial for two hundred dollars. She scrounged around and found eighty-seven dollars. I covered the rest. That's the last she thought she would ever have to take care of her father, and she didn't take the time to find out where he would be buried.

We went home. Ma was already back, and I noticed Winnie May in the corral. We chose not to tell Ma just yet. She was her sweet, kind self and told Suzanne all about her day. Suzanne listened in a daze.

It wasn't long before JJ pulled in with two sows and a boar in the back of his old pickup. He came bursting in the house, bragging about his day and how proud Pa ought to be if he kept this up. Soon thereafter Reverend Durham, John, and Sam came riding in. Suzanne's crisis got lost in the crowd until later that evening when Pa was back also. After dinner, everyone sat around the table and JJ dominated the conversation by telling Pa about his hunting adventure. I guessed no one got hurt.

In the midst of JJ's story, Ma turned to Suzanne and asked, "You look out of sorts tonight. Is JJ's story botherin' you?"

"No ma'am, we found my father dead today," Suzanne said quietly.

"No! No!" Ma said as she sat back in shock. "What did you do? What funeral home is he at?"

I thought I better kick in here. Ma definitely had everyone's attention. "Ma, we paid to have a pauper's burial for him. He's taken care of," I said.

"No, you cain't just do that. He needs to have a good Christian burial and send his soul off the right way," Ma demanded.

"Now, Ma, you settle down," said Pa. "This is her father and she did plenty for the guy while he was alive."

"Well, I never…"

"Ma! Leave it alone!" Pa snapped at her. I think that was the first time I had ever seen Pa raise his voice at Ma.

Suzanne stood up and, without looking at anyone, walked out the door. Alarmed, I stood up and watched her walk out, then I followed.

"Maybe it's time I moved on," she said.

"What you talkin' about? Ma'll get over it," I said. "They all love you like one of us; sometimes I think more. This is just kinda shockin'. They'll get over it. They weren't the ones that had to live with the guy. Cumon, give 'em a chance to learn and understand." I put my arm around her. She turned, buried her face in my chest, and wept bitterly. I thought her heart was going to break.

"I loved him the best I could. I never wished this on him," she said between sobs. "I was his princess when I was little. He used to take me everywhere. I wanted the dad I knew when I was little and I kept hoping he would get help. When he'd be drunk, he'd still call me his princess. Now he's dead because he thought his little princess had abandoned him."

"I understand," was all I said and let her pour out her heart on my chest. I loved this girl, and I swore to myself from that point on I would do anything to protect her.

Chapter Ten

Annie came to the house the next day as JJ, Reverend Durham, John, and Sam left for the day's hunt. JJ and Annie had spent the previous night feeding the dogs and cleaning up cuts and abrasions. One of the hounds received a two-inch cut on his foreleg as a result of getting too close to the boar just as Sam had tied its rear legs together. The other dogs were just scraped up from running through briar patches. Annie and JJ doctored them up with antiseptic cream.

JJ couldn't say enough about Thor's stellar performance. That dog had fearlessly gone after the two hogs Annie's other dogs had bayed, and he avoided getting a single scratch.

John had recently purchased a pit bull himself and brought his dogs along on this hunt. He had the bay dogs from previous hunting, but had lost a good pit bull when an infuriated boar caught the dog across the belly and threw him about ten feet. It killed the dog and put a damper on John's hunting until JJ came along. His dogs had flushed out a third hog.

The guys took off Friday morning, hyped up and planning on taking down four hogs by the end of the day. They knew they would have to go deeper into the woods and farther down the river if they expected to take down Ol' Lucifer. In fact, JJ took his rifle along this time. I knew he realized that the deeper he hunted, the greater the odds were of running into the old boar. He would never admit it, but I knew that, just like me, he had a deep, visceral fear of confronting this hog. It was emotional to him. He had a personal vendetta to satisfy.

I spent the day helping Pa while the girls went to town. I appreciated Ma and Annie taking Suzanne under their wing and helping her through her crisis. I knew she would open up to them. Girls have the ability to do that.

When they got back from shopping, they had a pile of packages and were talking, laughing, and kidding each other. I was relieved to see Suzanne's spirits high. I knew there would still be quiet, sorrowful moments, but this was a step in the right direction.

Late in the afternoon, the guys came riding home looking well-worn and saddle sore from a good, long day of riding. Looking at them, I wondered if they were ready for the third day.

Pa and I had spent the day in and out of the field getting welding supplies to repair a floodgate in one of the washes. The gate was designed to float open in high water and allow debris to flow under. Then, as the water flow would decrease, it would hang down to prevent cattle from climbing underneath the fence in the wash to escape to the other side. It had corroded, and the hinges along the horizontal base bar of the fence had broken loose causing the floating gate to torque and bend downstream. The cattle had found the hole and were using it to go in and out of the pasture.

Pa and I had put in a good day's work. We repaired the gate and were exhausted. We still had the livestock around the house to feed. I was complaining to myself until I saw the guys come riding in. JJ had already made one trip; I noticed two hogs lying and panting in the corral. Again, JJ had left Winnie May in the corral along with Rounder. Neither horse wanted anything to do with the hogs and were snorting and whinnying about it.

Sam pulled in the second time. They obviously had met their goal and had captured four hogs. The only casualty this time was Sam getting thrown off his horse. It seems he tried to head off a hog bolting from the dogs when they thought they had it bayed. Sam's horse got spooked by the charging boar and threw him. It had bruised his hip and shoulder, so JJ traded places and let Sam drive the truck in while JJ brought in the horse. Everyone put their horses in the corral and loaded the hogs in Pa's horse trailer. They headed home to nurse their sore muscles and prepare for the final hunt the next morning. JJ still had to run the hogs to the buyer. They made $300 that day—not bad for a day's work.

When JJ came dragging in for the night, we were all outside on the deck enjoying the cooler night and drinking some hot tea. He came out to where we were and plopped down. Annie got up and brought him a big glass of iced tea. He smelled of sweaty horses and human body odor.

"Well, we did it," he said. "We got our four hogs, but that's a hard way to make a livin'. The only thing I'm bummed out about, though, is I didn't have a run-in with Ol' Lucifer. He either left the county or is hidin' out purty good. I seen other hogs runnin' off from us, but I'd know if I saw Ol' Lucifer. He's stayin' low. I ain't givin' up though. Tomorrow's another day."

"You watch it and don't take any chances with that old hog," Annie warned him. "If you see him, just shoot him and don't try to be a hero and bring him in alive. He's killed before, and he'll do it again. You aren't any good to me dead!"

"I ain't gonna do anything stupid," replied JJ. "I know how fierce he can be. I won't even give him a chance. My 30-30 will stop him in his tracks."

The next morning, it was clear that the hunters had learned their routine well. They were up feeling fresh and out on the trail well before daylight. They knew they had a long ride to get to the far southeast side of the ranch. Neither JJ nor I had ever hunted or explored in that part because there were just too many wetlands and too much thick undergrowth to hike around in.

The day went by quickly, working with Pa, following the fence line, and looking for holes that had to be patched. Pa told me about his boyhood; hunting around here with his pa. "There was deer twice as big as they are now. We used to hunt for food by shooting the does or young bucks, not the trophies. Hunting just doesn't provide for natural selection where the biggest and strongest deer propagate their species. It's always the trophy ones that get taken out. Wild turkeys used to be thick in the lowlands too. Me and my pa would spend the night and hunt for a big turkey and bring it back to dress the Thanksgiving table." I could tell how much pride he had in this old ranch. Our roots were here.

Toward the end of the day, Pa and I called it quits and went to see how JJ had done for the day. Pa didn't say a thing, but I think he was anxious for JJ to find Ol' Lucifer and eliminate the underlying anxiety about this territory and bring peace back to the ranch. When we got back, there were no signs of anyone showing up. Apparently, they hadn't had the luck they did the day before.

They were still not home when evening came. A quiet anxiousness enveloped the house. Annie was the first to say something.

"Is it that far back into the southeast part of the ranch that it would take this long?" she asked, looking for a general reply and some comfort.

"They probably just got more hogs than they know what to do with," answered Pa as he got up and made his way into the kitchen. I think that was his way of not having to answer any more questions.

Twenty minutes later, we could hear clattering by the barn and corral. Annie jumped up and charged out the door. We all followed her. It was JJ, John, and the good reverend putting their horses in the corral. JJ was shaking his head, and they all looked muddy and somber. The first thing Annie noticed was that JJ only had three dogs and Thor wasn't among them. John's pit bull was looking pretty beat up with a couple deep cuts, and John was minus two bay dogs. I couldn't see Winnie May anywhere.

"What happened to my dogs, JJ? Where are they? JJ, are my dogs dead?" Annie demanded.

JJ turned around and just stood there with both of his hands dropped to his side and looking small for a big guy. The other two stopped and watched, but held their tongues.

"JJ, you answer me! Is Thor dead?" she shouted, now getting in his face.

He turned away, "Annie, please, they're dead—three dogs and Winnie May. My Winnie May is dead."

Annie stopped in her tracks, covered her mouth, and looked at JJ in total shock.

JJ sobbed. "Ol' Lucifer tore my horse to shreds. I barely escaped. Thor saved my life." He broke down.

Annie just looked at him for a moment. Then, her heart softened, and she stepped forward and put her arms around him. I had never seen him cry like that.

I heard him say, "She's been my faithful friend for eleven years, and that infernal hog tore her to pieces. And to rub salt in my wound, started eatin' on her soft parts, and all I could do was watch. I'm gonna kill that hog if it's the last thing I do and eat the whole thing myself!"

"Don't talk crazy. We need to just quit this hog hunting and find something safer to do," said Annie.

"No, you don't understand, Annie. This hog's killed enough. I ain't stoppin' until he's dead!" JJ declared with fire in his eyes.

"You're tired, JJ. Just come in and tell us what happened," Annie said quietly.

Chapter Ten

"Yeah, go on in, JJ. We've had a big day and it's church tomorrow. We all need a day of rest." Reverend Durham patted him on the shoulder, and John followed suit. JJ just went in while the other guys loaded up their horses.

When he went in the living room and cooled off, he rehearsed the whole story to us:

We spent most the mornin' ridin' to the southeast corner, fightin' the dogs the whole way. They desperately wanted to be set loose. We finally got to where the brush and briars was just too thick, and there was a deeply cut stream tributary with banks too steep for the horses. We had to weave around to find trail. Then we set the dogs loose. It didn't take long for 'em to lock on to somethin'; we had no idea what. It was so thick, it took us a while to find our way to the dogs. When we got there, we thought we'd found the mother lode. There were hogs everywhere in this swampy area. Best we could see, we figured there was ten or so hogs. They was all squealin' and snortin' at the dogs.

The dogs had them held up in a shallow swamp. We couldn't see too far through the cypress trees and all the moss hangin' down. I still had Thor, and he was cryin' and barkin' to be set loose. I just couldn't make up my mind which hog to set him loose on. I had no idea what would happen with that many hogs in one spot. I saw a purty good size sow and set Thor loose on her. He charged in and had her by the ear in no time. With this many hogs, though, the others turned on him. Suddenly, he had three hogs on him. He let go to defend himself.

I was so caught up in watchin' the dogs that I didn't see Ol' Lucifer comin'. John yelled at me. Then I heard the deep squeal. I turned 'round just in time to see a huge black form chargin' at me. His mouth was wide open with drool flyin' everywhere and two eight-inch tusks comin' at me. I could swear his eyes were fiery red. Winnie May spotted him and rared back to try to fight him. She came down hard on his haunches. I saw him stumble, and he squealed in pain. What I didn't know was that he took a good swipe at Winnie May's underbelly and cut it wide open. She backed up and rared up at him again. Ol' Lucifer was keeping his distance. I thought she had taught him a lesson. I was feeling bolder and proud of Winnie May's fightin' spirit. But as I was tryin' to unholster my rifle, she just rolled over on top of me in the muddy water. I scrambled out from under her and jumped up. She was crying and tryin' to get up. Then I saw it; her bowels were ever'where. I woulda shot her right there if I could, but Ol' Lucifer spotted me and came straight for me. I knew I was a dead man just like Grant. I didn't look. I just kept scramblin' in the mud to get to my feet. I just waited to feel the knifelike tusks at my back and his hooves on top of me.

It never happened. I was scramblin' to make it up a tree when another boar started after me. I barely made it. I turned around all soaked and shiverin' even in the heat. There was Thor givin' battle to Ol' Lucifer. Thor had stalled him enough for me to make it to safety. Thor had him by the ear, and Ol' Lucifer was squealin' so loud it hurt my ears. He swung Thor around and shook his head until Thor tore most of his right ear off. That was Thor's bad luck. In that fraction of a second, he had a mouthful of ear and couldn't defend himself. Ol' Lucifer attacked him and sliced right through his spine. Thor yelped and collapsed. Ol' Lucifer knocked him around like a rag doll, swingin' his head and slicin' him to pieces. Then Ol' Lucifer stomped and stomped him until there was nothin' left to stomp but a bloody mass of hair.

When he was done, he turned around and looked at me, shook his head, snorted, and pawed the ground. I could tell he had my number. I couldn't see the other two guys anywhere. I thought they were dead too. When Ol' Lucifer decided he couldn't get me, he walked back over to Winnie May and started feastin' on her abdomen. I couldn't stand it, so I screamed and screamed. I guess he finally got annoyed enough. He turned around and urinated all over Winnie May's remains and left.

I waited for a while then climbed down and ran for my rifle. I stood my ground, but the hogs were gone. Eventually, I heard the reverend and John yellin' from other trees. Seems they thought it was safer than on a horse and the horses could run for their lives.

I shot three times in the air to scare anything off that mighta still been around. John and the reverend came runnin' to me and we stayed as close as we could to each other on the way out. Any noise at all made us jump. Further out, I shot my rifle again to try to scare anything off.

When we made it to an opening, the other three dogs came runnin' up to us, lickin' us almost like they were relatin' to us and was glad to be alive and see us alive too. John lost a couple bay dogs, but his pit bull was alive.

We had to hike 'bout two miles before we saw the horses. They found a good place to pasture and looked totally content. We figured the hogs weren't anywhere around, or the horses woulda been able to smell 'em.

On the way home, the good reverend said to me, "I feel like we just hiked outta the bowels of hell, and I swear that big old boar had to be the biggest, meanest, ugliest animal I ever saw in my life. He looked like the devil himself in animal form. I've got to warn our congregation; there is something evil happenin' here."

I heard John say, "Ya know, Reverend, I ain't been to church for a long time. Tomorrow I'm comin'. We all coulda been layin' back there dead. I don't want nothin' more of this game. I want out."

"Well, I think you're a fool to get mixed up in it again.

That's a fearful story, and it could be you next time," I said to JJ.

JJ looked at me with hate and vengeance in his eyes. "I've had enough playin' around, and I ain't stoppin' 'til that boar's head is hangin' on my wall!"

"This is crazy talk. I'm not having any of this. JJ, if you're going to be fool enough to stick yourself in harm's way, I can't stick around to watch it happen," Annie said and got up to leave.

"Wait a minute!" he shouted at her. He paused to rethink what he just said. "To be more honest, on the way home tonight, I thought about trappin' instead and stayin' out of the way," he quickly offered.

Annie spun around and put her hand on her hips. "Well, that's more like a good plan. I do think that hog needs to be put down. I just don't want my fiancé put down in the process." She went over and sat on JJ's lap even as muddy as he was. She kissed him and said, "That was a pretty terrible thing that happened to you out there. I'm glad you're back safe. That's the way I like you." Then she kissed his dirty face.

Chapter Eleven

Ten o'clock sharp, the bell rang above the little white church. It was Sunday morning and everyone was feeling a lot better about life than the day before. My family was gone, and I stayed home and took care of the animals. Suzanne tried to talk me into going that morning, but I didn't want to. Religion was just there to make people feel good about themselves. It provided a good moral philosophy to live by. But, when it was all over, we all end up in the grave. I was fairly sure that's where it ended.

I worked on Rounder's hooves; cleaning and clipping them. The more I thought about Suzanne's invitation, the guiltier I felt for not going. I think she just wanted me there to be with her. So, I decided to join her. I figured she'd appreciate me supporting her. Even with my personal beliefs, I wasn't against religion. So, I dropped everything and went in to clean up.

I walked into church and Reverend Durham spotted me

and smiled. Suzanne and my family turned around and smiled at me. I sat in the back so I wouldn't interrupt anything. Suzanne got up and came to join me.

One thing that always impressed me was the reverend's way of using his life's experiences as analogies—like his hunting experiences. I guess he must have been quite affected by the events of the day before, because that's what he used in his sermon this time. If nothing else, his stories entertained me.

He started in about how swine have been written about in both Old Testament and New Testament times with horror and disgust. "Swine were looked upon as unclean and forbidden to be eaten. Many stories in the Bible use swine to represent disgust or degrading situations such as not casting our pearls before swine, or a deceitful woman is like a pearl in a swine's nose." The congregation chuckled at that one.

Then he related the story out of Mark in the New Testament where Jesus crossed a sea after teachin' the parable of the sower. "He went into the land of the Gadarenes and there he was met by a man with an unclean spirit among the tombs. No one could bind him with chains or fetters, and the man couldn't be tamed. The man saw Jesus from afar off, came to him, and worshipped him. Christ asked who the demon inside this man was and he said he was Legion because there was many of 'em. Jesus commanded the demons to quit tormentin' the man and cast them out. A herd of two thousand swine was near 'em and the demons asked if they could enter the swine. Jesus gave 'em leave and they did. The whole herd ran down a steep hill and drowned themselves in the sea."

Reverend Durham went on to say, "Swine are perfect, filthy animals for devils to possess. Our community is cursed with demons occupying swine bodies right here. Look at the death of Grant and Judge McNeil's boy and the strange disappearances of livestock around this area."

He recounted the details of their hunt yesterday; the near miss with that giant hog and how he could feel the presence of evil. He admonished us to repent and pray that this evil could be rooted out from among us because this was a way God was using to punish us.

He had us all scared. Judge McNeil and his wife were in the congregation. The judge stood up and asked to speak. The good reverend let him have the floor.

The judge scanned the audience for a moment. Everyone was silent. "Contrary to what the sheriff's department wants to believe, JJ Longbow came to me and told me that he thought it was the hog that killed my son and not anything that a human did. JJ said it was too similar to what he had witnessed when he was a kid, and hog tracks were everywhere. JJ was right. My son was tragically assaulted by a wild beast! It has to be destroyed before anyone else's child dies this tragically. The police want to stick to their story because they don't want to create hysteria in this area." He paused. "I'm offering two thousand dollars reward for anyone who kills that beast. I'm basing the identification of the hog on what the reverend told me late last night."

The crowd went into an upheaval of murmuring and talking. The reverend had to quiet everyone down. Judge McNeil sat down and let the reverend have the floor again.

The reverend challenged anyone who had access to traps or hunting rifles to seriously consider helping to eradicate this curse.

Church got out at one o'clock. My family all came home talking up a storm. Ma had already had a pork roast in the oven with lots of vegetables—how prophetic. I could say one thing about Sunday: It was the best mealtime of the week, and it was tradition to get everyone to sit down and eat together. Pa blessed the food, and everyone dug in. As we ate, we kept talking about the unusual sermon Reverend Durham preached.

Pa spoke up, "That hog is on our property, and I ain't lettin' a vigilante force on our land to end up shootin' each other."

"Pa, I met with the reverend afterwards and agreed to let him join me in trying to trap Ol' Lucifer," JJ said. "I'm gonna need some help, especially if we catch him. That giant's got to be nearly seven hundred pounds. We're goin' out sometime this week and buyin' the goods to make the trap. He says he knows an ol' boy down in Zapalla who can help us set it up. I think that's a better strategy than some vigilante force like you said. The reverend agreed with that too."

Pa looked at JJ with piercing eyes for a long moment. "Havin' the good reverend involved and tryin' to trap this beast is one thing, JJ, but Mrs. Durham pulled me aside while you were talkin' to him and Sam. She says y'all made a pact to get this hog and split the money. I'm here to tell you, JJ, you're not playin' with a normal animal. And you better have your keen senses about you and know when to pull out. I been in battle situations, and even though we're the strongest country in this world and know how to fight, sometimes we been in over our heads and we had to know when to pull out. You're an adult now and I ain't gonna tell you what to do. But if you don't play it smart, JJ, we're gonna be buryin' you too," Pa warned. I'd never seen him quite so cautious and nervous looking.

The weather had turned bad. It looked like a big one was blowing in. Dark clouds had formed a large squall line. Pa had us all out battening things down. There was a storm warning for Angelina County, and circular motion clouds had been spotted on radar that hinted at tornadoes. We drove the vehicles into the barn to avoid any damage if hail hit us.

Once we had everything protected, we stood and watched, fascinated as the almost-choking, hot humid day instantly turned into a cool breeze, and the cool breeze into serious winds. Suzanne wrapped her arms around me and snuggled, seeking protection from the storm. It didn't take me long to realize that she had a particular fear for storms. I didn't question her about it. I knew she'd tell me eventually. Things were starting to blow around, and the dust was picking up, so we decided it was time to get inside. To the west, thunder and lightning flashed and cracked continuously. Behind the lightning a solid, dark gray wall of rain was coming our way. It was a welcome relief from the dry weather we had experienced lately.

Soon the rain was coming down almost sideways, and the wind continued to blow. In a matter of minutes, the ditch in the front of the house near the road had swollen to almost full. We were experiencing a good three-inch rain all at once. It had turned completely dark. It was hard to see, except during the flashes of lightning all around us now.

"Shoot, this probably means I'm gonna get called out. This kind of weather always brings power lines down," said JJ, still looking out the window.

Annie had gone home to help her family get things secured. We were lucky. Except for the strong wind and a little hail, we didn't sustain any damage.

An hour into the main storm, JJ's forecast had come true. The phone rang. It was the utility service company calling JJ out. They said that North Lufkin got hit pretty hard. They didn't think it was a tornado, but very strong straight-line winds. Many power lines had come down and pole transformers had blown out. They needed him right away. He changed into his utility boots with pole-climbing barbs on them, threw on his yellow slicker, and headed out the door into the night storm.

JJ was gone until 8:15 the next morning. When he showed up again, he came recklessly speeding and spinning his tires into the driveway, driving somebody else's car. He slammed on the brakes, sliding to a halt. He could be easily heard outside cussing to himself as he was coming in. Ma had breakfast ready knowing he would be tired after being out all night.

She looked through the kitchen window and watched him throwing his tantrum. "I wonder what's wrong with JJ? He's sure out of sorts. And whose car is that? Usually he's so tired, he just drags in, eats a little, and goes to bed. He's in a rage this mornin'."

Just then he burst through the door almost taking the screen door off its hinges. He stomped in, threw his wet clothes down, and paced the kitchen floor.

"What's got you all balled up?" I asked.

He sat down. I noticed he was shaking. "My goodness, JJ, what's happened to you?" asked Ma as she came over and checked his body temperature. JJ answered:

I'm okay, Ma. Y'all ain't gonna believe this, but I swear on my own honor it's true. And I'm gonna have to call the sheriff here purty quick. I never did get to work. I took off outta here in a big hurry and got about four miles down the road headin' into Lufkin. It was still rainin' hard and it was dark. I was havin' a real hard time seein' the road. My wipers were goin' as fast as they could. Suddenly, my headlights shined on somethin' big in the middle of the road. I slammed on my brakes and veered off to the right onto the shoulder. As soon as my wheels hit the mud, it was over and the rear end slid into the ditch. The lights were shinin' in the air, so I still couldn't see what it was I tried to avoid.

I got outta the truck thinkin' it was just a cow or somethin' and lookin' to see how bad I was stuck. I stepped onto the highway, and there he was. I didn't even scare him off. Ol' Lucifer in the middle of the road chompin' on some road kill. He looked up at me, let out a loud squeal, and charged straight after me with his head down and his big mouth wide open. He scared the fool outta me! I about unloaded in my pants right there. I scrambled to get back into my truck and was in just as he assisted me shuttin' the door. He hit the truck so hard, he drove me further into the ditch and collapsed my door.

I watched him squealin' and shakin' his head back and forth. I'm tellin' you here and now, Billy, this hog's got my number. Why was he on the road just as I had to go by, and why did he hold me hostage in my truck? He squealed and he squealed. Then he started headbuttin' the truck tryin' to get at me. He went around the truck lookin' for another way in. I reached over and locked the passenger door. That may sound silly, but I was scared; and I didn't want him findin' any way to me. As he went around to the back of the truck, he jumped up and put his front legs on the tailgate tryin' to get into the bed. He kicked with his back legs and shook the truck, but wasn't able to get in. Then he disappeared for a while.

Ma, I was prayin' for someone to come and rescue me. I was hopin' anyone would drive by.

I was probably there for about two hours and scared to death to get out. I put the truck in reverse and tried to back out. I just got stuck deeper. I kept lookin' to see where he went when I saw some movement up by the trees. I knew he was still there just waitin' in the shadows.

Finally, a car came down the road and slowed down to see if anyone was in the truck. On second thought, I tried to signal him to just go on, but he stopped and got out to see if I was okay. It was still rainin' just hard enough to make it hard to see into the windows. I rolled my window down to yell at him to stay in his car. It was too late. He was out. He smiled at me and asked if I was okay. Before I could even answer, I heard the splashin' of that monster comin' after him. I stuck my arm out the window and screamed for him to go back, just as he was hit.

JJ's face quivered. He sputtered trying to speak:

Before I could stop him, Ol' Lucifer slammed him to the ground. I don't think he knew what hit him. I sat helplessly and watched as that black devil beast mangled that man before me. I cain't stand it. I'm goin' crazy seein' this and not bein' able to do anything about it. Billy, he tore that man into pieces. Then from out of the trees, five more hogs showed up. Between them, they feasted on that man's body, fightin' and snarlin' over pieces of him. They didn't leave nothin' but a few pieces of clothing and a bloody mess.

I sat there wet an shiverin' until the sun shown again and I could see what was in the shadows. Nobody else drove by. I got out and saw what was left of the man. I threw up right there at the sighta what those hogs did.

There was no way to just lift my truck or jack it

out of the mud. That guy's car was just sittin' there. I just got back in my truck scared and confused. I was just too freaked to even get back outta my truck. Finally, when the mornin' light was bright enough for me to see, I took a chance. I ran, jumped in the guy's car, and came straight home.

"Ma, you better call the sheriff and get someone out there right away," I said. "I'm goin' with JJ back to the scene. We need to get there before someone else stops and freaks out."

"No, I ain't goin' back!"

"Cumon, JJ, we need to go back. I know this is hard, but we need to be there," I shouted. Time was of the essence so no one would suspect JJ of any wrongdoing since his truck was there, and the guy's car was gone.

We arrived before anyone else and had time to look over the scene. The man had been killed on the asphalt, and there was a little mud scattered around from the hooves of the hogs. I squatted by the remains. Lying among the fringes of the mangled flesh was the man's wedding ring. I picked it up and looked at it. There was a family without a father now, simply because he stopped to help. I stood up and moved away from the smell and put the ring in my pocket.

Hog tracks were all along the side of the ditch. I couldn't gaze on the wretched scene any longer either. There wasn't much left of the guy.

A few minutes later, the sheriff's deputy arrived. He parked and stayed in the car, talking on the radio for an unusually long time. He stared straight at us. I became increasingly uncomfortable with the situation. After what seemed like forever, he finally got out of his car and asked us to step away from the scene. We backed off. He walked to the gore left behind and stooped over it with his hands on his knees. The body cavity had been completely devoured. The man's face was gone, as well as most of the extremities. It was obvious this young officer had never had to deal with this kind of scene before. I guess I was callous from what I had witnessed in Vietnam and as a young child. The deputy got sick, ran behind the car, and lost his breakfast. He ran back to his vehicle and was on the radio looking much more excited. He got back out and called us over.

"What happened here?" he asked in a shaky voice. "There's not much more than a bloody ribcage and scattered bones left."

"Hogs got him, sir," was all JJ answered.

"How? Why? What happened? I want you to tell me what took place here! Who is the guy? Is that his truck in the ditch?" the deputy demanded.

"Sir, slow down and let me tell you what happened," said JJ, now having a grip on the situation. He rehashed the whole story to the officer.

The officer just stood in amazement. "You know the investigators are going to have a lot of questions for you. They may consider this a hit-and-run manslaughter or something. You'll have to stay close to the house."

I could see JJ getting all worked up. "Yeah, isn't that the way things always get done around here? How can you call that a hit-and-run? You can tell somethin' ate him. I'll bet y'all still think Judge McNeil's kid was a homicide. I'm tellin' you, there's a beast in these woods, the likes you better pray you never have to face. I sat scared outta my head in that truck watching the whole gory scene and you're gonna put it off on me?"

"The animals may have gotten to him after he was hit," the deputy said quite unconvincingly.

Just then three more squad cars pulled up. We were asked to get into the deputy's backseat until they were satisfied they had asked all the questions they needed. Everyone that drove by took a close, careful look at us sitting in the backseat and shook their heads. I didn't think we looked like such criminals.

Annie and Suzanne drove up in Pa's truck and ran as close as they could to see us. The investigators stopped them and would not allow them any further. Annie cried hysterically. Suzanne comforted her and cried herself. They stayed there until the investigation was over and all the pictures were taken.

The investigator came to us to ask the same questions, after things were cleaned up, to have JJ tell his story again. The investigator asked if either one of us knew this man. We said we had never seen him before. He asked JJ to continue, stopping him every so often to clarify something. He would ask a question then walk over to the scene to see if anything verified the story. After a barrage of questions, he released us, but told us to stay in the county.

We walked over to the girls and rode home with them. When we got home, Pa was there and had heard the whole story from Ma.

Chapter Eleven

Pa looked at both of us sternly. "That's it, boys, we gotta do everything we can and take out that hog. He's just not natural. I think he's tasted human blood and likes it. He's not gonna stop killin' till he's dead."

"Leave it to me, Pa. I'm gettin' that trapper from Zapalla tomorrow," said JJ.

Chapter Twelve

JJ worked hard that afternoon to contact the trapper from Zapalla. He couldn't reach Reverend Durham, so he drove to his little house near the church. An hour later he was back looking angry and distraught. He said he had found Reverend Durham and his wife in the yard cleaning up the broken branches and debris from the previous night's storm. JJ had told him about the events of the night before and asked him for help to bring in the trapper and to capture Ol' Lucifer. Sally, the reverend's wife, went in the house as soon as they started talking hogs. The reverend watched as she walked off. Then he turned to JJ with a sheepish look. The reverend stated that his wife had given him an ultimatum to quit this dangerous sport or she would leave him. He said it was a good fight and that hog needed to be captured, but for the sake of his family he was staying out of it, and wished him luck. Disappointed, JJ asked him for the number of the trapper. He went and got it and gave it to JJ.

The trapper's name was Jonas LaRoache. JJ called him as soon as he got home. He was a big Cajun who had grown up trapping in the deep woods around Lake Sam Rayburn. JJ told him he would pay him three hundred dollars for a day's work if he would come immediately and help him construct these traps. Listening to JJ on this end, Jonas must have been pleased with the offer, because he said he'd be there in a couple of hours.

JJ chuckled to himself as he hung up the phone. He sat down at the table. "This guy's good, but he don't have any idea what he's gettin' into."

"He sounded purty impressed with your offer," I said.

"Yeah, funny how his voice changed to soundin' all authoritative. Those poor folks think of three hundred dollars like we look at a thousand," he chuckled.

Jonas LaRoache was right on time. It was mid-afternoon, and it was another hot and steamy East Texas summer day. This guy was quite the character. He looked as if he could have wrestled any hog, alligator, or whatever else stepped in his way. He was, to my best guess, in excess of three hundred pounds. He had a heavy black beard with braids tied off on either side of his mouth extending from the ends of his mustache. He was taller than JJ, making him at least six feet three inches tall. He wore a dirty white T-shirt with breakfast stains on it and a buckskin vest over his bib overalls. He had a necklace of boar tusk ivory, all of the tusks ornately carved with geometric designs. His hair was pulled back tight into a long skinny ponytail all under a flat top, wide-brimmed, brown leather hat.

Chapter Twelve

I walked outside with JJ to meet him and immediately noticed his body odor. He jovially introduced himself and stuck out his huge hand to shake with us. Not knowing which of us was JJ, the moneyman, he kept switching his attention back and forth between us.

"Oooh, I see you're brothers. That's easy to tell in the face, just one of you is more of a squirt than the other." He laughed tapping me on the shoulder. In comparison, I guess my five-foot eleven-inch frame was small. "So which of you is JJ?"

JJ looked at me then back at this jovial giant, who was still brandishing a big smile. "That would be me." JJ stepped forward to shake his hand. It was obvious Jonas was a hog hunter. Like the reverend, he was missing his pointer finger on his right hand too.

"Glad to meet you, JJ," he said as he shook JJ's hand with the same level of energy he had portrayed.

I introduced myself. "Hi, I'm Billy. Nice to meet you." He turned and nodded to me as he shook my hand. His hand nearly swallowed mine, being twice as big and very thick.

"So, you got hog problems around here too? The wretched things are takin' over these parts. They just breed too fast, and they're smart critters. You know you can train 'em easier than a dog, and they're faithful too," Jonas said nervously, trying to make conversation.

"We didn't bring you here to teach us how to make pets out of 'em. We have a problem; especially with one that's a man-eater. He probably weighs over seven hundred pounds," JJ informed him.

"Aiee! Seven hundred pounds. Ha, ha, they sure seem like that when they's on your tail, don't they," Jonas said trying to determine if we were exaggerating.

JJ looked Jonas straight in the eyes with a stone-cold expression. "I ain't payin' you to come here and kid around. Just last night during the storm, I got stuck up the road. A man stopped to help and before he got to me, this giant hog hit him so hard he probably never knew nothin' after he hit the ground. That hog devoured him right before my eyes, with a little help from some of his friends. And that ain't the first time I seen him do it. Me and Billy watched him kill and devour one of our best friends when we were just kids and I don't know if you heard about Judge McNeil's kid up the road…"

"That kid was killed by the same hog?" Jonas probed. JJ now had his attention.

"Yes sir, the very same one. And I'm tellin' you, he's real cagey and elusive," JJ added.

Jonas suddenly wasn't so jovial. "I been huntin' hogs fur goin' on twenty years now and I've witnessed how vicious they are even among each other. Their matin' rituals are brutal. What kind of hog is he?"

I spoke up. "He looks to us to be almost pure Black Russian hog. He's got a lean rear end and a long snout and is silvery grayish black."

"These Russians are especially vicious and fast on their feet," he said. He shook himself out of the fearful state he was succumbing to. "Well, y'all are payin' me to help you catch the beast; not stand here flappin' our jaws. But, I'll have you know, I ain't here to get myself killed. I've had too many close calls before, and I advise y'all that if we trap this bad boy, you better shoot him before you even get close."

"That's what we plan to do. I vowed to take this hog down. It's him or me, and I don't intend to lose," declared JJ.

Jonas went quiet and glared at JJ for a moment, then stated soberly, "Like I said, I been huntin' hogs for goin' on twenty years. They're smart animals. Some say they're amongst the smartest of the animal kingdom. Animals have souls too and, just like the Bible says, these are loathsome animals and I think they sense things. It sounds like this one has sensed your challenge. That's what I think. I don't want none of that. I'm here to show you how to set up a trap. I ain't here to help settle any vendettas."

"Let's get started then. We got a lot to do before sundown," said JJ.

Jonas had us busy gathering the supplies to build a good hog trap. We had several livestock panels around the ranch. We loaded them on the truck along with some flexible, wire fence panels and some metal fence posts. Jonas said he brought some bait. He went over to his truck and grabbed a tub of fermented corn mash. It smelled as bad as hogs do. In addition to the fermented mash, JJ wanted to stick a dead goat in the cage. JJ was convinced that blood would attract Ol' Lucifer more than the mash would.

We hauled all the materials as far as we could on the truck. The heat had dried out the roads except for the puddles. We made our way with the three of us stuck in the cab of JJ's truck. Jonas stunk so bad that, even though the air conditioner was on, I had to have the window down to even breathe.

We drove near the spot where JJ had seen the hogs. We didn't go in as deep, but we found a shady area near water and set up the panels. They hooked together with some solid pins through hinges. They were made to hold cattle kicking and leaning into them. The front of the trap was four-inch by four-inch grid fencing. We created a circular corral with an opening at one end. We closed that end by connecting the panels with bailing wire and used the steel fence posts to hold it in place. The front created a type of funnel where one side was out further than the other one. The other was flexed around a fence post and stuck inside the first panel. Since it was flexed, it pressed against the first panel giving away into the trap. The hog would have to push his way into the trap to get the food and it would spring closed behind him, creating no way out. It looked like an ingenious idea and a way to capture several hogs.

For the first time all day, JJ was excited. He envisioned this corral full with Ol' Lucifer and the other hogs that seemed to run with him.

"I can smell that reward money and the old hog goin' down. This is gonna do it," JJ said.

"What money?" Jonas inquired. "You holdin' out on me?"

"News ain't traveled that far yet? Judge McNeil offered a reward for anybody who slays Ol' Lucifer. After today I wouldn't be surprised if the reward money goes up," JJ announced. I couldn't help but think we just made a big mistake telling this guy.

He was putting the final touches on the trap and immediately stopped what he was doing, "How much is this reward?"

JJ stopped and, I believe caught onto what he had just done. "Two thousand dollars. Look, I'm not a greedy man. My intent is to stop the fear and danger this threat is holdin' over my family and this community. What happened last night is fixin' to hit the streets probably in tonight's paper. You tell a community that there's an elusive, man-eating wild boar out there, and panic is gonna strike. If this is gonna change the way you do things, then what do you want?"

"Aiee! Yeah it changes things. I ain't got a whole lot, and that money could solve a lotta problems for me right now. We're gonna catch that hog. We ain't givin' it up to some other stranger, and I garr-onn-tee there's gonna be a mess of people comin' to Angelina County from parts unknown all the way out from South and West Texas. Deer huntin's gonna look small in comparison. In fact, they gonna be so thick round these parts you're gonna think you're at a gun show. People are fixin' to get hurt, I garr-onn-tee."

"So, what do you propose we do different?" I asked, having tried to stay neutral so far.

Jonas smiled his big smile, "If you got the stuff, we need to set up a couple more of these here traps. Then we need to patrol them a couple times every day. If we don't, we're gonna lose him because of two things: Captured hogs will find a way out; and if another hunter spots your traps with somethin' in it, he'll steal it in no time."

"We ain't lettin' no hunters on our property and we're gonna patrol. The sooner we find this hog the sooner this is over," JJ naively said, a little overconfident. I could have easily predicted what happened next, knowing the state of mind JJ was in.

"Ha, ha," Jonas responded laughing at JJ's response. "You don't know city hunters, do you? Don't be stupid. People are gonna be in here like fleas on a dawg. Y'all got too much land here to patrol it all."

JJ's face got beet red. He walked up to Jonas, "You don't know me, buddy, but I been huntin' all my life and I don't need the likes of you laughin' at me."

It didn't take me long to figure out Jonas was a real scrapper. Lightening quick, Jonas shoved JJ so hard he went flying off his feet and landed hard on his back. It knocked the breath out of him. After he collected his senses, he sat up stunned. I knew I could disarm Jonas with a whole different approach if I needed to, but I thought JJ needed to eat a little humble pie.

"Hold it, guys. JJ, you paid Jonas to come and show us what he knows and you been bossin' him and snappin' at him ever since we got started. It's time to shut up and listen," I said, trying to disarm the situation.

Jonas just kept smiling and turned to me. "Thank you, Billy. You got smarts to compensate for bein' a little guy."

I just kept quiet and didn't let him rile me, although I knew that's what he was trying to do. A guy of his mentality tries to use physical domination to establish the pecking order. It became obvious to me that JJ's measly three hundred dollars had no effect on this bad boy any more after he heard about the reward. JJ stood up, dusted himself off, and cooled down.

"We need to work together on this. I respect the fact that this is your property and y'all can run me off at the end of a gun. So, I'm proposin' you let me partner with y'all, and we can split the money three ways," offered Jonas.

"No! That ain't right. We own the property, the traps, and we..." JJ started again.

"Hold it, JJ!" I interrupted. "The money ain't the main issue here. We got a hog to kill, and face it, we need help."

JJ just sputtered and kicked the dirt, walking away with his hands on his hips and looking at the sky.

"What do ya say, JJ?" I asked.

He kept his back to us. "Okay, do what you gotta do."

I paused for a moment then turned back to Jonas. "Okay, Jonas, we split it three ways, and we'll even give you an extra four hundred bucks for livin' expenses if you help us and we trap the big boy."

"I vote we elect this boy president," Jonas said, back to his jovial self. "If we're gonna catch this granddaddy, we need to get those other traps set. You gotta think like a hog, they can cover a lotta territory searchin' fur food. They ain't like deer. They cover a lot more territory, so we need to do the same with the traps," he continued.

"My first item of business as president is to bait this trap and get outta here before we cain't see nuthin'," I responded.

"I like him already," Jonas answered.

We baited the trap then jumped in the truck to head back. I got stuck in the middle with two stinky guys now.

After I couldn't hold back any more, I said, "Second item of business is y'all need to take showers. You're invadin' my oxygen space." They both laughed and ribbed me from both sides.

Chapter Thirteen

When we got home that night, Pa showed us a copy of the Lufkin paper. The man's death that JJ had witnessed was on the front page. They had a picture of JJ and me talking with the investigator. We didn't even know they snapped the picture.

The article said the man's name was Stephen Guseman, survived by three children and an estranged wife. He was returning home after spending a few days with his children. The paper told the story accurately and called the death an apparent wild hog attack. The article tied it to the death of Judge McNeil's son and listed us as witnesses. It became apparent the judge had stepped in and made it clear to the sheriff that he was doing no good trying to cover this up and not call it what it was.

In an interview, the judge made this statement, "I am declaring the hog problem in Angelina County an epidemic. Too many people are being killed or seriously injured in their interaction with the hogs. I have offered a two-thousand-dollar reward. In an emergency meeting with the county commissioners and the mayor, the county has tripled my offer, bringing the reward to six thousand dollars for the eradication and positive identification of a particularly large Russian boar known to be stalking this area."

In one way we were pleased. This took the heat off JJ. On the other hand, it meant that every hog hunter in the region would be out that week trying to get the reward money and shooting everything that moved.

We turned on the news at ten o'clock to see just how far this news was going to spread. To our chagrin, the interview with the judge was shown and, again, our names were mentioned. This meant there was a good chance the hunters would focus their efforts around, and as Jonas said, on our ranch. Trespassing and trouble with our cattle could get out of hand.

Jonas had gone back to Zapalla the night before and was back the next day armed to stay a while. The three of us spent the entire day in the miserable heat setting a couple more traps at strategic locations around the ranch. We were sure that if anyone was going to get the reward money, it would be us. Several of the ranch gates from off the main road had locks on them. Pa allowed us to give Jonas a set of keys so he could help patrol the area.

We went back to the first trap to see if we had any luck the night before. No luck, but the summer heat definitely made the aroma of the dead goat and the corn mash carry a long way. Hogs have a keen sense of smell, and we were confident they could smell this one if they were anywhere in the region.

We went home to clean up for the day and to get the sweat and trail dust off. Afterwards, I was ready to kick back and relax, when I noticed Suzanne was getting rather snippy and not her usual self.

"What are you all worked up about, Suzanne?" I asked, motioning for her to come join me.

"Oh nuthin'," she responded, looking away from me.

"Come on, what's eatin' ya?"

"I'm just tired too from a long day at work, being hit with a multitude of questions about the incident the other night and about the hogs. People ask me if I really think that's what happened or if I think it's a cover-up. Some people have no clue what's going on out here, and others, some of the older farmers, who are having hog problems of their own, welcome this massive hog eradication. They want to know the details of what happened.

"Actually, I think people around here are getting scared. They can't ignore it now that the judge has gone public on the news. I hate it, Billy. I'm sick of this hog stuff. It seems that as soon as I moved in here, all I ever heard you talk about were those stinking hogs. I almost think it was easier to deal with my father than to be here living in the shadows of a bunch of pig fanatics." She stopped, covered her mouth, walked to the living room picture window, and looked out.

"Whoa, whoa, Suzanne!" I stood by her side and put my arm around her shoulder. "I think what you need is to get outta here for a while. I think you're gettin' ranch fever.

You need a night on the town…and so do I. Let's get outta here."

She looked up at me, took a deep breath, smiled, and said, "You know, I think you're right. Give me twenty minutes." She kissed me on the cheek and was gone. I was exhausted, but I knew what I had to do. I had not given her much attention in the last couple of days, and I knew she still had unresolved issues in her own mind about her dad.

She was ready in twenty minutes just as she had said. My exhaustion disappeared. With her being around the house, I had taken her too much for granted. She was strikingly gorgeous. It reminded me how important it was even to me to keep our romance alive. I gave her a big smile and pretended to slick my hair back.

"Ma'am, would you be willin' to accompany me tonight?" I asked as I bowed.

She laughed and slapped me on the shoulder. I truly missed having the time to stare into her hypnotically deep-blue eyes.

"Are you hungry, ma'am? I know a quiet little place where we can be alone, eat some good food, and then burn it off with a night a dancin'," I said to her with my hand over my heart like I was trying to hold it in.

She smiled at me, "Now that's my man back. I'm starved for food and attention."

I treated her like a queen, opening all the doors for her. When we got to town, we were feeling good, laughing, and teasing each other like kids. We got to my quiet little restaurant/diner, but it was so packed we couldn't get in. The parking lot was full of horse trailers. We left frustrated and drove around town. Hunters with trailers packed with gear, four-wheeler all-terrain vehicles, and others with horse trailers were everywhere. It was sobering to see the frenzy that had come out of this.

Suzanne and I settled for an old drive-up hamburger joint. It was the only place not packed.

"This is insane, Suzanne. I'm sure the judge didn't know he'd be puttin' a lot of other people at risk. These are people from Dallas, Houston, and ever'where in between. From the looks of their gear, a lot of 'em have never even done this before and don't know what they're gettin' into. A lot a people are fixin' to get hurt," I said as we waited for our burgers.

"Its amazing what money will do, Billy. I'm really afraid for these people. They'll probably shoot each other," Suzanne said.

Our burgers, fries, and shakes arrived. They were the best tasting burgers we'd had for a long time. The place was old and desperately needed a good paint job, but the cooks there still knew how to make a tasty burger.

"When I was little, my daddy used to bring me to a place like this," Suzanne remembered.

I looked at her and smiled. I could see a nostalgic look in her eyes as she smiled back at me.

"Billy, I know I was coldhearted and insensitive when my father died. I've had plenty of time to think about it. My heart breaks to think that I never told him how much I really did love him. Sometimes I think that's why he drank. People never told him how much they cared, not even Mom. I see now that there were issues that weren't necessarily all Dad's fault. I miss the wretched man, Billy. I miss him terribly. And it breaks my heart to think how he died, probably thinking that nobody in the world cared anymore."

"It was a bad situation, Suzanne. But you did everythin' you could, and all you did is get outta harm's way. It does my heart good to know you really care. It shows me the sensitive heart you got there," I responded with as much empathy as I could.

"Can we go find where he was buried?" she asked. "I want to show my sincere, heartfelt respect. I'm ready for that now, and it will bring some closure for me."

"You betcha we can. Let's start at the police station," I offered. It was getting late, but it was worth a try.

We got lucky. The dispatcher remembered the officer who was on duty when Suzanne's father died. He was disarming a hot situation at the Trail's End Bar.

"Sure glad we didn't go there tonight," I remarked to Suzanne. "I mighta' had to do some quick steppin' and I ain't talkin' about dancin'."

The officer told the dispatcher that the body was turned over to St. Augustine's Parish. They have a special burial place for transients and paupers. That was more than Suzanne could take. She broke into tears thinking of the people her father was buried among.

"You're doin' the right thing here, Suzanne. Quite frankly, your dad don't care who he's buried among," I said trying to console her. She looked at me, wiped her tears, and just rolled her eyes at my poor choice of words.

"That would be Father O'Malley if you wanna contact

him. The government offers them a certain amount of money to see to their burial," the dispatcher said.

She gave us the address, and we drove over to the old, central part of town. We found the little, old, stone church with the adjoining father's quarters. We were a little nervous, considering it was a little after eleven o'clock. Hesitantly, we knocked on the door. It was quiet just long enough for us to decide to leave. As we turned to go, the door opened. We turned back to see the gentle face of a middle-aged, sandy-haired, slightly balding man. He couldn't have been over five feet four inches and was at least fifty pounds overweight.

"Can I be of help to you young folks?" he inquired, looking at us with his mouth partly open.

"Uh, yeah, Father? This is Suzanne Wesley. Her father died a couple weeks ago, and we couldn't afford a funeral. We were told he's buried here somewhere," I responded.

"Would that be David Wesley?" he asked.

"Yessir, it would."

"Come in. I will show you on a plot map where he is located," the father offered.

We went in. It was a quaint little place, but full of high-quality, stately, leather furniture. The walls were beautiful hardwood panels, ornately trimmed in highly crafted hardwood. For light, he had numerous candles burning instead of using the fixtures. This added a soft glow to the Christus statues and art along the walls, which practically told the story of Christ's whole life in pictures. He went to the large bookshelf that covered a complete wall, pulled a binder down, and laid it on the desk. As he thumbed through it with his reading glasses on, he asked us how Suzanne's father died.

Suzanne looked at me somewhat hesitant. "He drank himself to death, sir," I answered for her.

"That is usually the outward result. Actually, sir, what I'm asking her is, what caused him to drink himself to death?" probed the father looking over his reading glasses.

I thought the father was awfully bold. He was speaking as if he now owned David's soul. I didn't know if it was right or not. Then I figured probing into people's souls was what he did for a living.

Suzanne looked at me, still hesitant. I looked back critically like she didn't have to answer. She then took a deep breath and responded anyway, "We usually spent the Fourth of July together alone. This year, I wanted to spend it with Billy, my boyfriend, and his family. Afterwards, when I went home, he got angry and tried to beat me up. He hit me a couple times and I was out of there never to come back. He killed my mother the same way." I could see the anger welling up in Suzanne.

"Maybe we need to stop this," I suggested, defending her. She just looked at me unsure of what to do.

The father patiently turned to me and asked, "Is this something you're going to require of her? To keep it penned up until she explodes, maybe at you? Families of the people who get buried here usually have unresolved issues and like to have a priest that, most likely, they'll never see again and that they can let it out to. If they can get it off their chest to someone who is impartial, it leads to resolution."

Chapter Thirteen

"Oh," I responded, a little confused. I looked at Suzanne. She silently shook her head like it was okay.

"Well, maybe this can be a good thing," I conceded.

"Continue, my daughter," he said signaling Suzanne to continue.

"I hated him for being a drunk. It destroyed his life, and I didn't want any part of it. When I left, I was angry and afraid. I wasn't ever going to go back again. Now that he's dead, I deeply regret that I never told him I loved him. Reflecting back, I don't think my mother or anyone else did either. He died an unloved man." She placed her face in her hands and wept bitterly.

"My sweet daughter, know this: He can feel your love even now while he is in the bosom of our Lord and Savior Jesus Christ. He is loved and feels it now more than he has ever known. He is resting in peace, my daughter." He stood up and took her hands. "Put your trust in your Savior. Your father is okay." He smiled at her and helped her up. I automatically stood up too. "Now go. Visit with your father at his grave and tell him how much you love him. The angels will carry the message to him."

She was deeply relieved and smiled at the father. "Oh, thank you, Father. You have lifted a tremendous burden off my shoulders."

We walked to the door and bade the father good night. I didn't say anything, but I thought to myself how that episode was an interesting play of human psychology to comfort her. How does that father know or even care where her father ended up? To me it was just a patronizing way to make us feel better about the inevitable dark nothingness of death, but this was not a time to express my opinions.

We walked from the father's quarters on a little path, beautifully landscaped and trimmed with many varieties of flowers and rose bushes. Up the path about thirty feet was a wrought-iron gate and fence. Our path was brightly lit by a three-quarter moon. We made our way through hundred-year-old head stones to the rear of the cemetery. A whip-poor-will sang its song over and over in the trees not too far away. In the spot shown to us on the map was a mound of dirt and two small survey flags. We stood in silence for a few minutes.

Then Suzanne spoke. "Daddy, I want you to know that I love you with all my heart. I don't know why it took until you died for me to realize that all you wanted, like any of us, was to be loved and respected." She kissed her hand and patted the mound. She turned to me, "Thanks for being patient with me and for being here tonight." She then led the way out.

Chapter Fourteen

Over the next few days, Jonas and JJ became good friends. Every night Jonas joined us at the dinner table and ate like a horse. It made Ma proud to see him enjoy her food so much. Jonas looked like a Viking with his big, black beard and braids. We learned to enjoy having him around and enjoyed listening to his backwoods stories. JJ told the family all the hunting and trapping techniques Jonas had taught him. Jonas especially won Ma's approval when he quoted from the Bible showing he'd had a good, Christian upbringing. Pa just sat back and took it all in.

When Jonas had gotten comfortable with us, he shared that he had been a marine and had spent two tours of duty in Vietnam in the late sixties. He said, in all soberness, that he really didn't like to discuss that episode in his life, but that's why he liked living by himself outside of Zapalla. I just listened until Ma spoke up and told him I had been in Vietnam too. I had a new respect for him now. I could tell

Pa did too. We had gone through similar traumatic events in our lives. He became part of our family's inner circle.

At first, Suzanne and Annie were scared of Jonas. As time went on though, Suzanne would pitch in with the rest to tease and joke with Jonas. I could tell Jonas had taken a special liking to her in an honest sort of way. He turned out to be quite a gentleman underneath his rough exterior.

It was quite the opposite with Annie. She was a proud person, and Jonas's jokes somehow offended her. She told JJ that she wouldn't come around anymore as long as Jonas was present. So, later in the evenings JJ would excuse himself to see Annie. That was okay, because JJ used it as an excuse to see Sam, Annie's father. Sam had bought JJ a new quarter horse so he wouldn't lose a good roping partner. JJ would spend the evenings training his horse.

Almost every night the local news covered the ongoing saga of the man-eating hogs. The county brought in some biologists who were experts with "suidae" as these experts would refer to swine. They had heard stories in history about wild hogs turning on men, but they knew no other time when there had been cases like this before. The coverage was replete with hunters who had either been injured in a shooting accident or were injured by an angry hog.

Several hogs had been brought in for the reward. Many were huge by normal standards, but nothing matched the official description of Ol' Lucifer.

JJ and Jonas had reenlisted me to patrol and escort hunters off our property. They were busy doing the same. They hadn't seen any hogs in their traps yet and were getting frustrated. Jonas said it was because there was too much activity in the area. When it died down, the hogs would be back.

Three weeks passed, and most of the hunters had given up and gone back to their city jobs. Many hogs had been harvested, but Ol' Lucifer was not among them.

Our job became much easier. Trespassers weren't a problem anymore. With that behind us, JJ went back to work, and Jonas stayed around to check traps and put out bait. He had learned from JJ where the deer feeders were located, and he kept them stocked also. The deer population had dwindled significantly due to the high traffic, but they would be back too.

The weather was constantly sultry. The stock ponds had become glorified mud holes, and natural, fresh food was difficult for wildlife to find. Jonas kept saying that these drought-like conditions would bring the deer and the hogs back to the feeders.

Pa and I spent our days touring the ranch and securing its borders where hunters had torn down fences, cut holes, and broken locks off gates. We had to do a lot of field welding.

It had been a pleasure spending time that summer with Pa. I got to know a completely different dimension of him. I was surprised to learn how much Indian culture was instilled in him, such as his love of the land, respect for all animals, and his uncanny insight on life. He was a Christian, but in a nontraditional sort of way. His form of worship came from feeling a part of the land and all of God's creation. This was in contrast to Ma who, in her own rightful way, shared her faith through constant volunteer work at the church. I admired both perspectives and appreciated how it created a holistic unity in our home. This was the atmosphere I wanted for my own eventual home.

After a hard day's work on one particular, badly damaged gate, which looked like it had been rammed to break the chain, Pa and I dragged in for dinner. Everyone was there. Ma had made an exceptionally good three-layer casserole. We sat around the table making small talk. Jonas said the deer were coming back. He had seen a group of four does, a young buck, and an older one. They were at the feeder. He said he spotted some fresh hog scat around one of the traps, but nothing had attempted to get in. He said he knew they were getting hungry though.

While we were sitting around feeling fat and relaxed, Pa announced that he was going to make a little trip to the south pasture and make sure the cattle were secure. I offered to go with him, but he asked me to feed Rounder and the chickens instead. I got up and went out at the same time he did. He drove off and I went about my business.

I was in the barn with the light on, talking to Rounder and feeding him, when I heard a noise around the corner, outside the barn. I stopped to listen. I heard it again, so I grabbed the pitchfork expecting the worst. I sneaked up to get a look. Everything was silent. I crept closer to cautiously peek out. Suddenly, a large image jumped in front of me making me step back and raise the pitchfork to do battle. The image let out a loud scream, "Gotcha!" It was Suzanne. She had come to join me.

"You scared the bejeebers outta me! You could get hurt doin' that!" I snapped at her. I was glad I was not closer to the door where I may have seriously hurt her. I stopped and collected myself, then laughed and gave her a big hug.

"I just came out to keep you company," she said as she snuggled against me. Aware of her sweet innocence, I realized she still didn't fully understand the danger of my volatile reaction to a sudden scare. I just put my arm around her, and we walked back to Rounder's stall. I went in, finished feeding and talking to him, and on the way out Suzanne blocked my path.

"Nice rear you got there, cowboy," she said with a sly look.

I dropped the feed bucket, wrapped my arms around her, and we began to passionately kiss. We had been very good to each other, but that night alone in the barn was a real temptation.

Our passionate moment was shattered by gunshots in the distance. Concerned, we stopped what we were doing and listened. The breeze was blowing just right, and we heard faint screaming, which alarmed me.

"Suzanne, that's comin' from where Pa was headed." We both got nervous and decided to check it out.

We ran in the house and I yelled to JJ that Pa might be in trouble. He jumped up from his cozy spot in the armchair in the living room, put on his boots, and we disappeared. We ran outside and jumped into his truck because he stored his rifle there. I grabbed it off the gun rack in case we saw something.

The first two gates were closed. Pa taught us to always shut them behind us. We came to the third gate that opened into the south pasture. Pa had been keeping young heifers isolated in this pasture. We drove through and I shut the gate. I got back in and we started moving, then JJ stopped.

"You see what I see?" There at the periphery of the headlights a cow was down. It was still struggling. We ran to it. It mooed pitifully. Then we saw it; the cow's belly had been slashed open and the poor thing was suffering. Out of compassion, I put a bullet in the back of its skull.

My mouth went dry. "Is this what I think it is, JJ?"

"Yeah, I'm afraid so, Billy. This is the work of Ol' Lucifer or one of them runnin' with him," JJ said, staring at the dead cow.

"Cumon, we best hurry and find Pa," I said not being able to hide my cold fear.

Without a word, we jumped in the pickup and both of us were shaking at the thought of what we might find. We slowly drove forward where the road bent around some trees heading into a draw. We went down in, bounced around, and came up the other side. Just as our headlights broke over the hill, we saw Pa's red pickup. We didn't see anyone in it. The pickup was still running. We got out and I immediately shot two shells in the air to scare off anything that might still be lurking. My heart was beating out of my chest.

There, lying in front of Pa's truck, were two more heifers—dead. They were attacked the same way. One looked well eaten, the other looked as though it was just randomly killed. They had already been shot in the head. We guessed that must have been the shots we heard when Pa put them out of their misery. In the periphery of the headlights, we spotted another large motionless figure. I cautiously walked to it. It was a dead hog that had to be about three hundred pounds. It looked like Pa had shot it through the neck.

"It looks like Pa got one of 'em. I wonder where he got off to?" asked JJ.

"I wonder if he's chasin' another one down," I said trying to be reassuring.

"This just ain't right, Billy. I'll go honk Pa's horn and you listen and see if you hear him yell from somewheres."

I stood with my gun ready, waiting for any movement in the headlights and feeling extremely vulnerable. I heard the truck door open, then...

"No, no! Pa, wake up! Billy, help, Pa's bleedin' to death. Come on, Pa, wake up!"

I ran to the cab. Pa was lying on the seat and wet darkness was all around. I turned on the cab light and was taken aback. Blood was everywhere—on the truck seat, on the floor, and dripping out of the cab. It was coming from his left leg around his groin.

I yelled, "Pa, please don't be dead!"

I felt his neck for a pulse. JJ took off his belt to make a tourniquet. Pa's face was ghostly white, his lips were purple, and his eyes had already glazed over.

"JJ, it's too late. He's dead. His artery's slashed. Looks like a hog did it," I mumbled in shock.

JJ dropped to his knees and wailed like a child. I wailed too and dropped down where we both cried in each other's arms. Our pa, the anchor of our lives, was dead. We couldn't do it; we couldn't bring Pa home. I drove and could barely see through the tears. I was so full of hate and rage, I would have taken on that beast bare-handed if I had to at that moment. JJ said it had to be one of the smaller hogs, considering the fact that the truck wasn't beaten up.

When we got home, we were shaking and swollen-faced.

Ma ran to us. "What's wrong? Where's Pa?" She knew before we told her. She dropped to her knees and wailed, "No! Not my sweet love! Why, God? Why him?" She cried hysterically.

JJ got out of the truck, stood her up, and embraced her as she cried. I got out, came around, and held them too. We stood there in the night, a pitiful trio.

Suzanne was the only one composed enough to call the sheriff's office and tell them what had happened. When they arrived, Suzanne went out and pointed them in the right direction. Most of the night was spent with the confusion of flashing lights from patrol cars, ambulances, and a tow truck.

The sheriff himself came in when it was all cleaned up. "Mrs. Longbow, we just want you and your family to know that we're truly sorry for your loss. Your husband was the most honest, levelheaded man I knew. It was positively identified as a hog attack. I actually thought we had cleaned this area out. We're going to take him to the Carroway Funeral Home unless your wishes are something else."

"Yes, please do that," Ma said still clinging to both JJ and me on the couch.

Sleep didn't come easy that night. The horrible scene of Pa dead in a pool of his own blood played over and over relentlessly in my mind with ever-present, demon razorback hogs lurking in the peripheral darkness on the edge of the headlight beams.

Chapter Fifteen

"Jack Longbow Sr. was a good Christian man and truly one of the kindest I know. He is survived by his wife and two sons. He was never financially wealthy. His wealth was his good family. All he understood was hard work. His claim to fame was that he was a wonderful husband and father…"

Reverend Durham's eulogy of my pa faded in and out as the entire scene replayed in my mind. I pictured myself shooting the hog over and over. The little church was packed and steamy-hot even with the ceiling fans spinning and the little window air conditioners running at maximum cool. Jonas actually came in a button-down pressed shirt and black jeans. JJ and I wore black suits and white shirts. Annie and Suzanne sat right behind us. They looked especially beautiful in their black dresses. Ma sat between us and wept quietly.

The funeral procession to the cemetery was very long. It

was probably the first time my pa ever got a Lufkin Police escort. At the cemetery, we stood in the hot sun as the good reverend blessed the grave and Ma threw in the first shovel of dirt. It was so permanent. There was no victory in this, just six feet of dirt. I looked at Ma; she looked so old and frail. Who was going to provide for her now? Who was she going to spend her autumn years with? She would probably immerse herself in church and community work. My guess was JJ would stay and run the ranch. It was a perfect transition for him and Annie after they got married. I would probably sell my portion to them since I had no desire to stay around. I wanted to go to college in the fall, then move off to bigger and better things.

After we laid Pa to rest, everyone stood around consoling Ma. JJ and Jonas quietly came to me and handed me a note. We walked off a little from the crowd. He and Jonas looked at me as I opened and read it, "I hereby swear upon my father's grave that I will not rest until Ol' Lucifer and his legion are dead, thus ridding this scourge upon our community."

The thought ran through my head as I pondered the note, "Why had this scourge focused on our community? Why had it taken my pa? Is it some kind of test? My parents have always been God-fearing folks, and for the most part, so was this community. Or, was it just that the marble settled in our slot in life's roulette game? I passed the note back and told them that I would help in any way I could, but I didn't believe I had to sign a pact. They looked at me a little angry, then as if to make a point, they signed it in front of me.

Chapter Fifteen

Ma invited people to come out to the house for the wake. We got home and the people started showing up with food. When it was over, nearly a hundred people had come through, offering their condolences. I had never shaken so many hands before. Really, all I wanted was my own family, so we could grieve in peace. I still didn't like to be around people and got nervous in crowds. We were left with a big mess to clean up.

We all pitched in together. After we had taken care of that, we crashed in the living room. That's when it hit us. Pa wasn't there anymore and never would be. I looked around at all his memorabilia and realized he would never touch any of it again.

Suddenly, JJ jumped up. "We got cattle to feed. C'mon, Billy, get changed and come help me." We looked at each other. I could see the fear in his eyes. It was the same as mine. We had no idea what we would find, and dead cattle were still lying out there. I got up and changed. We jumped in JJ's truck and drove to the barn to load some hay bales.

While we were loading, JJ looked at me. "Are you thinkin' what I'm a thinkin'?" he asked.

"You scared what we'll find out there?" I responded.

"Yeah, for the first time, I'm really scared. Not so much about runnin' into the hogs, just a general fear of impending doom. You know what I mean? I just ain't ready to die," he said.

"JJ, that's just what we felt like each time we had to go fly a mission in Vietnam. I thought nothin' could ever make me feel like that again, but this does," I said.

"Yeah," was all he said.

We worked in silence from that point on.

With the truck loaded and the sun low in the sky, we hurried so we wouldn't be caught in the darkness and not be able to see what was coming up on us. When we got to where the cattle were, we threw several bales to the bulls and steers, then drove to the heifer pasture. I don't know why it surprised us, but when we got to the first dead heifer, there was hardly anything left to drag off and bury. I could smell the pungent odor where the hogs had urinated on the carcass to mark their territory. I thought how revolting that was; knowing they probably ate her where they urinated too. We just left it alone; it was stinking badly after being out in the hot sun for a couple days. Through the draw and up the other side we found our herd. They came running. They were obviously hungry. They surrounded the truck as we threw the bales out. We could see the other two carcasses. They were rotting and had not been touched. We drove over to them and again, I could see where they had been urinated on. The hogs intended to come back and claim their harvest.

"Why don't we drag these two over and put 'em in the traps," JJ suggested. I thought that was a good idea, and it would get the hogs away from our herd. I mentioned to him that the carcasses looked like they'd been marked by being urinated on. He told me how he watched Ol' Lucifer do the same to Winnie May. To me, this meant the carcasses would be even more enticing in the traps. JJ thought it was a good idea. It had gotten too dark to do anything more that night though.

The next morning, the first item of business when Jonas

arrived was to get the tractor and move the carcasses. Jonas agreed that these marked carcasses would be enticing bait; especially for Ol' Lucifer if they were his own markings. It was a messy job, but we worked together and got the job done. In the process, enough blood and fluids escaped from the carcasses to leave a trail to the traps. We were proud of ourselves. We thought we were really on to something this time.

JJ, Jonas, and I were like little kids that night. We were sure we would capture something. The next morning Jonas showed up early, and JJ and I joined him. We drove to the first trap and, lo and behold, there were two young boars in the trap. They were not the least bit concerned about being in the trap until we drove up. They had spent the night feasting.

Jonas walked to the trap and the boars went into a frenzy, ramming the livestock panels, squealing, and trying to find their way out. Every so often they would ram where we were standing to try to warn us to stay away. JJ didn't show much mercy. He pulled out his 30-30 Winchester lever action, what he called his field gun, and shot them both. We dragged them off and left the bait as it was. Each one weighed about two hundred pounds. Between the three of us, we threw both of them in the back of the truck.

The next trap was empty, so we decided to take the two hogs and use them to bait the third trap. We laid them in the trap and eviscerated them to cause the aroma of fresh flesh to spread throughout the area. Afterward, we called it a day and headed back to the house.

When we got back, Annie was waiting at the house,

standing by the door. JJ jumped out, excited to see her. She didn't respond to his excitement. Jonas and I decided to leave them alone, so we went in the house. I looked out the window and saw that JJ was upset. Annie turned and headed for her car. JJ grabbed her gently to stop her. He said something to her and she just kept shaking her head and saying, "No." Then she got in her car and pulled out. JJ was slapping his thighs and shaking his head; then he rubbed his face and came in.

"What was that about?" I asked.

He stopped in the doorway, looked at me for a moment, then came in and plopped down at the table. Jonas just stood blocking the light from the living room into the kitchen.

"She said that she cain't handle any of this insanity anymore, that it's startin' to affect her life too. She said she understands what we're tryin' to do and when it all settles down maybe we can get together again. The sad part is, I really don't care right now either. I do, but I don't. I just couldn't pay her the attention right now that she deserves. I just don't care about nothin' but justice for the loss of my pa," he asserted in an unusually angry, but almost hypnotic voice.

"I know where she's comin' from. We check the traps then just live for the next day to see if we caught him. I don't even know what he looks like, but I got this big, monstrous image in my mind with foot-long tusks. I have to keep tellin' myself that it ain't like that," Jonas said. He wasn't much comfort, but it was true.

It got quiet after that. No one had anything to say, so we

just wandered around the house feeling like a dark shadow had been cast over us since Pa was gone. I knew there were chores to tend to, but I just didn't care. Things around the ranch were looking unkempt. If this didn't end soon, this ranch was going to fall to pieces.

Late that afternoon, Ma came in. She looked angry and distraught. I asked her what happened. She sat down in the living room and broke into tears, "Even people in the church are cold and don't understand. They think I should just get over the loss of my husband in a week and everything should be okay. I still hurt so bad from missin' him. Church should be one place I could go for peace and solace, and that's where I am hurt the most. They say coldhearted statements like, 'Well, now that Jack's laid to rest you can bring closure to this and let the healin' begin' or 'This is when your faith will be tested to see if you'll turn your life and service over to Christ.' I already know these things, but comin' from them, it just sounds shallow and heartless, especially when they just go back attending to their business like their statement just solved the world's problems. None of 'em have even come here to see me or find out how I'm doin'. And I been to all of their houses in time of need. I hate 'em all."

"Whoa, Ma." I'd never heard her ever say a negative word about anyone. I walked over, sat on the arm of the chair, and hugged her. She laid her head in my lap and cried. It ripped my heart out to see her suffer so. I stroked her graying hair. I told her I loved her and would always stay close enough to stay in her life. I told her that something those folks didn't have was two strong boys to take care of them and maybe they envied that.

I went to pick up Suzanne at work and explained the general melancholy mood at home. I told her what Annie had done. She asked how Annie could be so heartless. When we got home, we all sat around until the cobwebs filled our heads. Jonas crashed on the couch. It looked like the center of the couch was going to touch the floor. In normal situations, it would have been quite comical, but I was too numb to be humored.

Suzanne gave it up and kissed me good night. I admired her as she strolled off. She turned around quickly as though she knew I was watching, winked at me, and slowly shut the door.

We all went to bed. I lay there alternating between fantasies of ramming a spear into the side of Ol' Lucifer and him turning around to take one more slash at me; and seeing Suzanne's sweet face. Suzanne was the only consolation I had these days. I woke up out of my fitful slumber and cried again at the realization I would never have another one of those lazy, summer talks with Pa again.

I got out of bed and went downstairs to get a drink. I opened the fridge and stood in front of it in the sweatpants that I usually slept in. I reached for the ice water. As I did, I felt arms slide around my waist. I turned around. It was Suzanne.

"Cain't sleep either, huh?" I asked, looking deep into her eyes.

"No," she simply said, resting her head on my chest.

"Yeah, I just cain't get Pa outta my mind. I'll never see him again," I said.

"I just lie there and I can't get you outta my mind," she said to me almost like a child.

I looked at her in total silence as my heart raced. I hugged her, feeling like if I were to let her go, she'd disappear too. Then I kissed her with more passion than I have ever kissed anyone in my life. I could feel her melting in my arms. She stopped, took my hand, and led me to the living room. We snuggled in each other's arms in the love seat, snickered at the funny sounds Jonas was making, and talked for a while until we both fell asleep.

The sun shined through the window and warmed my face. I woke up, Suzanne was snuggled against me, and I was about to fall off the love seat. I started to get up, and she grabbed me and tried to hold me down. I stayed a moment longer, then got up and quietly walked to the kitchen to go to my room. Ma was sitting at the table with her cup of coffee. She looked up at me and said, "Good morning, Billy."

"Hi, Ma," I responded. She smiled at me mildly and went back to her coffee. Not another word was said.

After I got dressed, I met Suzanne in the kitchen. I convinced her to call in sick. After all this stress, I just wanted us to spend the day together. She excitedly agreed and, although she felt a little guilty, she made the call.

It wasn't long until JJ stumbled through the kitchen to wake up Jonas, who was still snoring away.

"Come on, Jonas, this could be our lucky day."

Jonas dragged up and wiped his tired eyes. "Yeah, this could be our lucky day; our lucky day to spend drivin' around smellin' dead animals," he said somewhat sarcastically.

In half an hour they were gone, and so were we.

Chapter Sixteen

Suzanne and I enjoyed a big breakfast at the 24-Hour Grill. We laughed and talked about anything and everything. It felt good to put the stress at home behind us. After breakfast, we made our way to the Lufkin zoo. It was a small zoo in comparison to the Dallas or Fort Worth zoos, but it was relaxing anyway.

One of the two, huge hippos had given birth and we were entertained by the interaction of the mother with her baby. I turned to Suzanne, "Do you think animals have souls?"

"Oh, we used to argue that in school. Of course they have souls. Every living thing has a soul."

"How are you so sure?" I retorted.

"That's why God gave us a Bible, silly. When it talks about creation in Genesis, it says that God created man in his own image. Then later he said there was not a man to till the ground. Then God said he created every plant of the field before it was on the earth and every herb before it grew. I also believe he created every animal for this earth before they came. He created them spiritually before he placed them here physically. Therefore, all animals have souls." She spoke with such simplicity and certainty. For the first time, it made sense.

"You know, I never heard it explained like that. I always believed it; I just didn't know where to turn to prove it. Well then, some animals just have a bad spirit, just like some people."

"Yes, that's why some horses are just ornery all their lives," Suzanne said.

"Well, yeah, but I'm talkin' about Ol' Lucifer. I believe he's just evil."

"Right, but let's not go there today, alright?" she asked kindly while wrapping her arm around my waist. "Can I ask you a rather probing question?" She looked serious.

"Sure, my thoughts are your thoughts. Shoot," I said trying to keep the atmosphere lighthearted.

"Why is it you say you don't believe in God when at the same time you ponder questions like that? You really do believe in God, don't you," she asked slyly, but sincerely.

She stumped me for a moment. Then I answered as honestly as possible. "I know you won't agree with this, but I think religion is man's way of tryin' to find purpose in a chaotic world and keep from goin' crazy from the insanity around him. I think Jesus was just an old carpenter who had decided he had enough of this eye-for-an-eye Middle Eastern stuff and tried to change the craziness. I respect him for tryin'. Suzanne, I spent a year in 'Nam seein' the craziness all around me and watchin' people who are suppose to be civilized kill each other in brutal ways, and others killing themselves. I said to myself, there ain't no God in this."

She looked at me totally unaffected, smiled, and stated, "You can't fool me. I know you believe in God. You're just mad at him. That's okay. I've been thinking and listening since my father died. At first I felt like that. Then, I realized that one of the greatest gifts God has given us is free agency; the ability to make our own decisions. He created this world with a lot of randomness. We set our course by the decisions we make and are affected by the decisions others make. The difference between people who find joy in this life and people who don't is their attitude. Nobody can take your mental freedom away. That's the right to let go, forgive, and move on."

I stood in total silence for a while. I could tell Suzanne was getting nervous and thought she had offended me. Eventually, I smiled and said, "That's why I love you. You're so optimistic even after all you've been through. You've definitely given me some food for thought." I didn't commit myself, but she had hit a nerve.

"Talk about ornery spirits, let's go see the 'gators. Now that's ornery," I said changing the subject.

After our stroll in the zoo and around the park, we ate a light lunch and caught the matinee.

Things were looking pretty good between Suzanne and me. I knew I loved the girl and I knew she loved me. That made all the rest of my problems seem insignificant.

By evening, we were feeling good as we headed home. I wanted to get home early enough to take care of the chores and check on the cattle that had been neglected for days. I asked Suzanne if she wanted to ride out with me. She said she'd enjoy that. When we got home, we saw Ma, with her apron on, standing at the screen door waiting for us.

"What's the matter, Ma?" I asked as I went around the truck to open the door for Suzanne.

"JJ and Jonas haven't been back since first thing this mornin', and they always come back for lunch. Jonas wouldn't skip lunch," she said, still looking off with a concerned gaze.

"Me and Suzanne were gonna feed the cattle. While we're out, we'll look around for 'em. Most likely they ran to town for somethin'," I suggested, trying to ease the tension.

We went to change into some work clothes and I played out all sorts of scenarios in my head. I didn't want to consider the worst case.

Suzanne and I went to the barn and loaded the truck with hay. She did a great job stacking as I loaded the bales. We spent our time talking about having to cut hay again fairly soon; the pastures were getting knee deep in Coastal Bermuda grass. As we worked and talked, though, somewhat in denial to ourselves, there was an underlying uneasiness in both of us that wasn't going to be satisfied until we saw JJ and Jonas again and made sure they were okay.

Shadows filled the thick, green piney woods around the perimeter of our pastureland as darkness threatened. On the way to feed the cattle, we drove by the third trap. Nothing had changed except that the horrific smell of death had gotten worse. We continued on to the second pasture and passed the place where we had found Pa dead. I pointed out the spot and the dead cow we couldn't haul off.

We unloaded the truck quickly, letting the cattle rip the bales apart. I was anxious to get to the other traps. We backed out of the second pasture and went to the second trap. Things looked the same there too. To get to the first trap, we had to hurry while we still had a little light. We drove through the wooded section that divided the far south pasture from the rest. Cottontail rabbits were in abundance and darted across the road in front of the truck. When we broke out of the woods, we spotted JJ's truck way down at the other end of the open area near where we set the first trap.

"There they are, down there, fooling around with that trap," Suzanne pointed out.

I got a knot in my stomach. I couldn't see anyone moving around. I didn't say anything yet. Then, as we cautiously drove closer, I spotted Jonas sitting in the cab of the truck on the passenger side. I breathed a deep sigh of relief. It looked like he was just waiting for JJ to finish something. I wanted to honk in my relief, but I knew they'd be angry if I scared anything off.

As I drove up to the passenger side, I asked Suzanne to roll down her window so we could talk with Jonas. We drove next to him, and I noticed he wouldn't look at us. He never moved his head, as though he didn't realize we were there.

"Jonas! Hey, fatso!" I yelled, thinking I'd get a response then. He just stared forward. His lips were moving, and he was lightly rocking. I leaned back and got a knot in my stomach as I realized something was terribly wrong. JJ's rifle was missing from his gun rack.

"What's goin' on here? Where's JJ? This doesn't feel right," I said, glancing at Suzanne.

She couldn't take her eyes off Jonas. She looked puzzled and scared. I opened the truck door; she quickly snapped around, "No, Billy, don't go out there. Something's dreadfully wrong. Please, I don't want you hurt!"

"Suzanne, my brother's out there somewhere—probably needin' my help. You stay in here, and if anything happens, you head straight back to the house."

She was shaking now as she scooted over to the driver's side. I kissed her to ease the tension.

I walked around the back of the truck and discovered the grizzly scene laid out before me. One of the livestock panels was knocked down and blood was all over the rear window and the bed of the truck. The truck cab headspace was partially collapsed and the tailgate was down. I knew something terrible had taken place, but still no JJ. I looked closer to the ground and saw the rifle lying there and a trail of blood leading into the woods. JJ had been dragged off. Suddenly, I was so sick and galled by the dreadful thought of what may have happened to my brother that I threw up. I had never done that before.

I ran to JJ's truck and yanked on the door. Jonas had locked both doors and still would not respond to me. I opened my truck and pulled the tire wrench from behind the seat. I smashed the window, which did cause Jonas to snap out of it. He screamed and cowered away from me.

"Jonas! Snap out of it. What happened here? Where's

JJ?" I screamed. He started crying and was babbling something.

"Jonas, it's me, Billy." I reached in and slapped him. That brought him out of it.

"Billy, Billy, get in here. He'll get you too. Hurry lock the door!"

"We gotta find him, Jonas. Come on, help me!"

"No, no, leave me alone. It ain't safe out there. Hurry! Get in before he gets you!" screamed Jonas in a quivering, insane voice.

It was sad to see such a big man reduced to a broken-down, insane mess. What had he seen? I opened the door and yanked on him. It was like pulling on an old, stubborn bull.

"You gonna just let JJ die out there?" I yelled.

"Billy, he's dead. I saw Ol' Lucifer drag his limp body off. He was dead," Jonas said.

"Gimme the flashlight under the seat. I'm goin' after him," I barked.

"No, Billy, please don't. Just wait until daylight," Suzanne screamed.

"That's my brother. I let too many people down before, I'm not leavin' my brother," I snapped at her.

I started toward the back of the truck. Then suddenly, everything went dark.

Chapter Seventeen

What seemed like days later, I awoke in a daze on the couch in our living room. I looked around at Suzanne and Ma sitting in the armchairs looking at me.

Suzanne stood up. "Oh, thank goodness, I didn't kill you."

I reached for my head and felt a major sore spot. I had a splitting headache. "What did ya do to me?" I asked. "My head feels like it's ready to explode."

"I'm sorry, but you just wouldn't listen to me," Suzanne replied. "I had to react fast to keep you from going into those woods after JJ. So, I jumped out and grabbed the tire iron you threw down and clubbed you on the head," she said apologetically.

"What day is this? How long I been out?" I asked.

"You've only been out for about an hour," Suzanne replied.

"Well, then where's Jonas? And what about JJ? How'd I

get here?" I asked getting alarmed again. I sat up and then my head pounded even more.

"Jonas gave me a little—very little—help dragging you into the bed of the truck, and then I made him get in your truck. I brought him home and we called the sheriff."

The screen door squeaked and banged against the wall. In came a tall lean deputy. He looked too young to be in uniform. He had a blonde handlebar mustache. If he was trying for the tough sheriff look, it didn't work. Actually, he looked very compassionate.

"Ah, um," the young deputy cleared his throat. We all turned our attention to him.

"May I sit down?" he asked.

"Oh, by all means, please sit here." Ma pointed to the armchair where Suzanne had been sitting and Suzanne sat by me.

"Mrs. Longbow, we found your son's body. I've already called for the coroner to come." He stood up and walked over to Ma. "Here is his watch and some keys. We'll take him to the funeral home for you."

Ma cried hysterically. "Oh, how terrible. My poor son. Oh, how could this happen?" Everyone sat there dumb-founded, too uncomfortable to say anything.

"Mrs. Longbow, I just want you to know, I played basketball with JJ. He was a good friend of mine in school. I always respected his even temper."

Ma stopped and looked up at the deputy, "Who are you? I kind of recognize you."

"I'm Officer Ryan Edwards. I played center, and JJ usually played a guard," he said.

"Oh yes, I do remember you," said Ma.

"Well, I better go and wrap things up. By the way, the big guy, Jonas, has been taken to the hospital for observation. He seems to have suffered major trauma and had an emotional breakdown," said Officer Edwards as he stood up and politely excused himself.

I followed him out to get more information on what they had found. When we got out the door, I asked him, "What did you actually find? What condition was he in?"

He looked at me somberly, pausing as though he really did not want to reflect on it again. Then he spoke quietly, "That musta been a mighty big hog to tear that trap panel down like it did. We had dogs down there and they followed the trail of blood. It led to a pond and disappeared. We searched around the pond until the dogs picked up the trail again. Then we followed it for another hundred yards or so. When we found his remains, not much was left other than some clothes and a few skeletal parts. The hogs devoured his whole body, bone and all. I never knew...I never figured hogs could do that. All we could do was gather the remains and put them in a bag. Billy, I'm tellin' ya, the bag wasn't very big, if you know what I'm sayin'. I didn't want your Ma to know the details. It's goin' to haunt me for a long time."

I shook my head and banged the screen door with my fist. I walked back in the house, paused in the living room entryway looking at Ma. She sat there looking so small and vulnerable at the end of the couch. I had never viewed her that way. She was staring at nothing, looking defeated. I went in, sat by her, and put my arm around her shoulder.

She turned and gently wept on my shoulder. I said nothing.

The next morning, I got up after another fitful sleep and found Ma in her now usual place: sitting at the table drinking her coffee and staring into space. I sat by her and didn't say anything for a long time. Finally, she looked at me and gave me a weak smile.

I leaned forward and gently asked, "What do ya wanna do, Ma?"

She was silent for a moment. I could tell she hadn't gotten much sleep, if any, from the exhausted look in her eyes. She then said, "I cain't afford another funeral and I don't think I could handle another one emotionally after your Pa's. I thought about this for a long time last night. I want his remains cremated and scattered here on the ranch. He loved this place and would have rightfully taken over in Pa's place."

That was fine with me; however, I had to suppress my surprise because I didn't think she believed in cremation. I considered it a thoughtful gesture, and I think she understood better than I had thought the condition of JJ's body.

Over the next few days, I took care of the logistics of JJ's cremation and tried to insulate Ma from all the nonsense people would say and do.

During this time, the sheriff hired additional men and dogs to go after the big hog. The men took the dogs to where JJ was killed to pick up the hog's scent. After several days of intense searching, the sheriff came to our door. I answered.

"Billy, can I speak to you concerning your brother?"

"Yes, sir." I stepped outside on the porch with him.

"Billy, we spent a solid week now intensely searching for that hog. The dogs have gone crazy many times, but haven't been able to find anything. We searched into the deep bayous and tributaries, and the trails just get too convoluted. We saw lots of hogs, but just not the right one. I would think with all the dogs and noise, we've scared everything out of here and into the next county. I just want to say I'm sorry. We tried and now it has reached the point that it's just too much of a strain on our budget to continue. I'm really sorry. I was sure with our manpower, we would have found him."

I looked at him like a defenseless child. "Okay. You did your best. This hog just ain't normal."

He looked at me a little perplexed and left. I went in and bore the news to Ma and Suzanne.

The next morning, Ma, Suzanne, and I went to the funeral home to be there when they cremated JJ's remains. Later that day, Suzanne and I quietly scattered the ashes from the little rock outcrop where JJ and I used to always come.

We stood there for a long time, then I turned to Suzanne, "Me and JJ used to come here and ask each other questions about the world and dream 'bout what we'd do when we grew up. I looked up to him and loved him so much." Suzanne hugged me. We stood quietly gazing out across the tributary. As I did, for a brief moment, I recalled vividly the whole incident leading to Grant's death.

This thought reinforced the conclusion I had already arrived at. "I'm goin' after Ol' Lucifer. If I don't, eventually he's gonna get me too," I angrily said to Suzanne.

"Please don't. Let Judge McNeil announce the reward again and bring in the hunters. Maybe this time someone will get him," she pleaded.

"Suzanne, the sheriff's posse did a thorough job and now this is personal. No one's killin' that devil but me. He and I are gonna have a comin'-to-God confrontation, and only one of us will leave the meeting," I told her.

"You don't need to do this. There are other ways besides putting yourself in harm's way," she pleaded.

"We already went that route, Suzanne, and a lotta folks got themselves hurt. I don't wanna see anybody else get hurt. I know this animal, and I don't need a bunch of inexperienced hunters spookin' him outta the territory, because he will be back."

She paused and then said, "I guess you don't get the hint. I love you and I don't want to stand around and watch you get taken from me," she said.

This struck me hard. I gazed into her deep blue eyes. "I love you too, Suzanne. I won't die. This one time in our life I need you to exercise that strong faith a yours and pray for me that I can put this scourge to rest."

She gazed back for the longest time, then the tears began to fall. "I think I'm beginning to understand now. There's something bigger than us going on here. I will. I'll pray for you, Billy."

We walked back hand-in-hand in silence.

The next day, I began my mission. I was determined to do this right. I was going to put things I had learned to survive in Vietnam to work here. First thing, I went to the library and researched what I could about the characteristics and history of hogs.

In my research, I discovered that hogs have been a terror and a prize trophy for noblemen in Russia and Western Europe for centuries. History is replete with stories of how Russian noblemen would plan hunting parties to go after wild Russian Razorbacks. They already hunted with dogs even back then. The hunting party would get themselves in the middle of a mess of hogs and be run up trees and dogs would be killed. The artist's drawings of the time humorously depicted scenes of men scrambling up trees, dogs flying, and angry boars standing them off.

I read of another time when an Irish prince went hunting with his father, the king. They went out boldly with their hunting party to combat the wild boar, which they believed to be the incarnation of past war enemies. In a particular hunt, the party came upon a particularly mean boar that ran most of the men up trees. To show his bravery and determination, the prince stood his ground. It was a foggy morning, and the prince had spotted the boar in and out of the fog. He could hear the squealing and snorting getting louder. He drew back his bow while he stood beside a tree. The fog parted for a moment, and he spotted the angry razorback. The fog closed in again. The prince shot into the fog and heard the painful squeal. Sure that he had killed the boar, he went running toward the sound. To his horror, he found that he had shot his father.

Knowing it was an accident, but not being able to allow the prince full freedom, rather than execute him, they banished him from Ireland in a boat without a rudder.

The stories intrigued me, but they weren't much help. I needed facts about hogs' characteristics. I came upon a "Feral Hogs of East Texas" study in the collegiate section. It turned out to be good material. I learned that they are smart animals that can outwit most predators and that they love to bed down in the thickest, most undesirable locations. I learned that they are opportunistic omnivores and will feed on what's most available. They have a keen sense of smell allowing them to find even small food morsels buried under a foot of dirt. They are very destructive to pastures and farms because of their rooting habits, and they need water nearby. It can be hot, but they need water. This was an important characteristic if I was to go to them.

Their mating habits are vicious too. A sow can bear young twice a year and can have up to ten in a litter. When two boars pair up to fight for sows, they will face each other nose to nose, then using a side sweeping motion of their heads, they use their razor-sharp tusks, kept sharp by two opposing teeth that rub against each other each time they bite or chew, to slash each other's faces and shoulders until one boar gives up. The battle can get very bloody. Because of this mating habit, boars develop shields of scar tissue and cartilage along their necks and shoulders. This feature makes the animal very difficult to kill with arrows.

I found out that early explorers such as Hernando Cortez and Hernando de Soto introduced hogs to America. These hogs were the domestic kind. In the early 1930s, the Russian wild boar was introduced. I was surprised to learn that significant populations existed in California, Florida, Oklahoma, and Hawaii as well as Texas. We weren't the only state plagued with this animal.

I had enough hog research for the day. I had learned what I needed to know. So I decided to stop by the hospital on my way home and visit with Jonas. In the back of my mind, I hoped he would be stable enough to perhaps join me. I had to admit I was scared of what I had to do. I really didn't care about the reward anymore. I went in to see Jonas in the hospital. He was glad to see me.

"Aiee! Billy, I'm glad to see ya'. I was wonderin' if ya'll gave up on me." He stood up from his bed and, towering over me, he slapped me on the shoulder as he took my hand and shook it.

"How can we forget 'bout a big teddy bear like you?" I asked smiling back and joining in on his lightheartedness. He had two chairs in his room, so he directed me to where we could sit down. Jonas' chair groaned under his weight.

"Whatcha been doin' with yourself in here, Jonas?"

"I just been sittin' in here bangin' my head against the wall an' antagonizin' the nurses. You know, the way I normally am at home," he said with a big smile as he looked up over my shoulder.

I looked back too. Then quietly he said, "We're bein' watched. They got a camera up there an' they record ever'thing I say."

Uncomfortably, I turned back around. "Well, you seem to be doin' a lot better than when I saw you a few days ago."

He smiled ruefully, then leaned forward, making the chair squeak again. "What can I do for ya, Billy?"

I leaned forward putting my forearms on my thighs and

met his gaze with a serious but soft look. I spoke softly, "Jonas, I'm goin' after Ol' Lucifer myself."

He leaned back without saying anything. He started to get shaky and would no longer hold eye contact with me. I could see the rosiness draining out of his cheeks. He looked at the camera with his mouth partially open. He smacked his lips a couple of times as if his mouth had gone dry, then he spoke softly:

We went out like we had fur the past week, ho-pin' we mighta got somethin'. When we checked the two closer traps, there was nothin'. Our hopes dropped for another day until we got close to the first trap we set way down by the swamps. We could see somethin' movin' between the slats of the livestock panels. I turned to JJ and told him we got somethin'. When we got closer, we could see his back over the top of the panel, so we knew we had somethin' big.

We pulled up to the trap and started cheerin' be-cause we knew we had Ol' Lucifer. I sat there amazed. I never seen anything like it, I guar-onn-tee. He was a beautiful animal fur his kind. His hair was black and kinda silvery on the tips.

JJ grabbed his gun off the rack and said that now he was gonna give him his just deserves. We both got out and by this time, my heart was beatin' in my neck. I remembered that animals could smell fear and I was preoccupyin' myself at settlin' down— tellin' myself it's just an animal.

Chapter Seventeen

We walked to the trap, and I just stood there with my mouth hangin' open. I never thought a hog could grow that big. His tusks had to be eight to ten inches long, curved up and back toward his eyes. Sure enough, he was missin' one ear. It was definitely Ol' Lucifer. He just stood there facin' us, pantin' real fast and his nose just a twitchin'. Ever' so often, he'd let out a little snort. JJ cautiously went around to the side and Ol' Lucifer shuffled around with him, keepin' both eyes on him. I knew JJ was lookin' for a good side shot through the heart, so I moved the other direction. Immediately Ol' Lucifer shuffled around to face my movement. This time he started snortin' like he was gettin' nervous.

Jonas was now wringing his hands and had developed a tick in his face. Suddenly, the door burst open and a doctor came stomping in wanting to know what I was doing. I told him I was trying to find out what happened out there and how my brother died.

"Sir, I can't allow you to go any further with this. Jonas just isn't ready to talk about it. He hasn't told us a thing," said the doctor.

Jonas stood up still wringing his hands. "No, Doctor, I wanna go on. I, I owe it to Billy to tell him so he won't hate me for abandonin' his brother," he insisted.

"Well, okay, but we're going to monitor the conversation," said the doctor.

"I don't care. I guess I'm gonna be a star on TV." A little try at comic relief from Jonas.

After the doctor left, Jonas sat down, took a deep breath, and let it out with his lips puckered almost to a whistle:

Anyway, where was I? Oh yeah. When the hog turned to me, the hair along the ridge of his back stood straight up. I knew he was gettin' ready to fight. Then everythin' gets confusin'. I don't know if Ol' Lucifer charged me first or if JJ shot first, but he charged me and hit the livestock panel hard. I fell back in total fright. After the shot, I heard the hog squealin' that horrid ree, ree, ree, like nothin' I ever heard before. I think JJ musta grazed him because before he could get off another shot, that hog charged the panel again. JJ came runnin'—yellin' at me to see if I was okay. This time the panel fell on top of me. Snortin' and squealin' and wild with anger, Ol' Lucifer broke a couple of my ribs where he stepped through the panel goin' over the top a me.

I saw him goin' after JJ. JJ ran to the truck screamin' fur help. He threw the rifle down and ran around the truck. Ol' Lucifer stopped just for a moment, picked up the rifle in his mouth, and snapped it in two. I rolled out best I could from under the panel to make a dash fur the pickup and got in on the passenger side. JJ ran around the truck, dove into the bed and climbed up on top of the truck cab. Ol' Lucifer went right up the front after him. JJ jumped into the bed of the truck tryin' to get over to the driver's side.

Jonas broke down shaking and in tears now.

Billy, ya gotta believe me, there wasn't nothin' I could do. Lightnin' quick, the hog ran around an' jumped into the truck bed. I turned around in fear and saw the giant had JJ pinned up against the back of the cab an' was slashin' him to pieces. JJ screamed for a moment an' tried to grab his head, but that laid him right over them razor-sharp tusks. That hog disemboweled him right before my eyes, swingin' him around like a rag doll. It never let off until JJ was a bloody heap. I couldn't see anymore outta the window 'cuz it was so covered with blood. I watched through the rearview mirror. He dragged JJ down outta the truck, then dropped him and came after me. I locked the door and he rammed the side of the truck three times. Each time, he'd back off, shake his head, snort and do it again. I was startin' to see daylight around the edge of the door. I figured if he does it again, I'm a dead man. He finally stopped, went back to JJ's body and dragged it off into the woods. Next thing I remember was wakin' up in here.

I been to 'Nam and I ain't never seen somethin' so gruesome. Billy, please believe me, there wasn't nothin' I coulda done.

He wept like a baby. I stood up and went to him. He grabbed hold of me and cried. I've never seen such a big hunk of a man broken down to tears like him. I let him cry for a minute, then pushed his shoulders, and moved him back.

"Jonas, you stay here an' get better. Nobody blames you. I got business to take care of."

Jonas understood what I meant.

"God be with you, Billy. Don't go gettin' yourself killed too."

"I won't, Jonas. I won't." I left him there still weeping as I walked out.

Chapter Eighteen

After a good night's rest, I wasted no more time. Suzanne had gone to stay with one of her girlfriends; she didn't want to be around to see me go. I pulled out my old camouflage clothes from my army stash. The familiar smell of canvas caused a flood of memories, good and bad. The camies were crisply folded in my duffel bag, untouched since I got home from Vietnam. I put on my boots and painted my face. When I came out, Ma looked at me in horrible surprise. She knew what this meant.

"So, you're goin' after him?" she asked in a reserved voice. She had a defeated look to her as she placed her hand on her chest and plopped down in her kitchen chair.

"Yes, Ma. I ain't sittin' around anymore to watch the people I love die. I have lived in fear of this beast almost all my life, and I'm not allowin' him to do to any other family what he's done to us," I said as I continued gathering my things.

"Son, I know I cain't stop you. As much as I fear for you and anguish at the thought of losin' my last loved one, I feel deep in my heart you're doin' the right thing." She paused for a moment, then continued. "I know you're angry with God, but for one time please turn your life over to him to help you come back safely," she pleaded.

I stopped, nodded my head in agreement without looking at her, and then proceeded to the gun closet. The old cherry wood cabinet had quite a selection of guns. Pa always kept them clean and well oiled, but as long as I knew him, he never used them. I pulled out his Browning 30-06 with the three to nine power, variable scope. He had different grain-size bullets in the drawer below. I rummaged through and found the heaviest grain, a 220-grain slug. "That should have good knockdown power," I thought. I took ten shells and put them in my pocket. In the drawer was Pa's favorite bone-handled hunting knife. It had a scrimshaw carving of an elk head on the handle. If anything could bring good luck, it would. One other tool I needed was my old military shovel.

As I headed out the door, all loaded up, I heard Ma say, "You're my only son and all I have. Please, come home again."

I saddled up Rounder to shorten the long trip to the other side of the ranch. I was headed deep into the bayous. It was a blistery hot day, and I was overheating in my camies. I knew I needed them to keep the bugs off me, but not right now.

I swayed back and forth to Rounder's walk; watching him flip his ears every so often to shoo away the flies. I was in no hurry. I patted Rounder on the neck. He was sweating as bad as me. "We been through a lot together, ain't we, ol' buddy. Help me out with this one and you can pasture the rest of your good years away."

Rounder knew the trail well. We finally arrived at the point where I needed to let Rounder go to keep him out of harm's way. I got off, tied the reins behind his neck so they wouldn't get in the way of his grazing, and sent him back home.

It was a miserably hot day and it was quiet in those thick, green, piney woods except for the sound of cicadas cyclically rising to a roaring buzz then totally shutting down. I could hear birds chirping and arguing with each other. Then, a scissortail flycatcher swooped down, caught a grasshopper, and flew back in the tree. It was so dry I didn't have to worry about chiggers eating me up.

Our pastureland was on higher ground sloping off to the dense forest. There were mild depressions where the runoff began to gather. As I followed one of these depressions into the deeper forest, the slope became steeper leading into the swampy area below. The depressions became more deeply incised. I soon came to a confluence of a small creek and found myself in a deeply cut creek bed with eight- to ten-foot walls. The banks were almost vertical, caused by the erosion by heavy spring rains through the soft sand and clay layers. I could see leaves and debris caught in the tree branches several feet above my head and recognized how fierce this mild little creek could be during a heavy rain.

I spotted fresh hog tracks where they had been running up and down the creek bed. I felt anxiety building in my gut as I imagined myself trapped in the creek bed not being able to climb the vertical walls if I were to come upon Ol' Lucifer. I took deep breaths to calm myself down. Where water was seeping from the creek bed walls feeding the creek, the hogs had made wallowing holes that had been well used. The trunks of the small trees were worn smooth where hogs had used them for rubbing and scratching. Time was on my side, so I took it slow. When I broke out into the flatter, swampy areas, I found scat and tracks. The area wasn't so much swamp as a series of wetlands.

I walked around the wetlands to where I saw wallowing holes in the shady muddy areas. They looked fresh. Chances are I scared the hogs out, but only temporarily. I walked a little further, and the evidence was increasingly abundant. I was now in hog country.

I knew my scent would be the first thing to give me away. I brought the shovel to dig a foxhole that I could stay in to avoid my scent traveling in the breeze and to stay out of sight.

I found a shady spot and started digging. The heat exhausted me by the time the hole was big enough to lay in. The ground was cool, and I soon fell asleep with the rifle beside me. I woke up, looked around, and still saw nothing, so I continued digging until the hole was big enough for me to stand up in.

It was late afternoon when I heard something. I couldn't see anything yet. A few minutes later, four sows appeared out of the heavy thickets at the mouth of a small creek bed, got into the shallow water, and lay down. They would take turns jumping up in bursts of energy and run around throwing their heads back and forth and splashing on each other.

After becoming refreshed, they were about to wander off when they all froze. They heard something that I couldn't. A moment later, a boar trotted in from the north. Just as he got close to the sows, another boar burst out of the thicket behind me. It scared the wits out of me. He had to be four hundred pounds. I was sure he would run right over me, but he passed five feet to my right. I held stone still. He didn't even acknowledge me. I had no idea these hogs were so close around me. They must have stayed bedded down until they thought I was gone.

The first boar slowly made his way around the wetland to the sows. The sows were bunched together, seemingly to protect themselves. The first boar looked more like a do-mestic-bred hog. It was big, round, and had large, black and white spots. He had a shorter snout and a curly tail. The other was a mix with a longer snout and a straight tail.

When the first boar got too close, the second hog charged him. The first didn't even flinch. He simply turned to face the other head on. I knew I was going to witness a good fight. Suddenly, as though they had both heard the same signal, they began slashing at each other, flailing their heads back and forth. They both let out ear-piercing squeals. Blood flew from their necks and faces. The smaller hybrid jumped up trying to get to the bigger one's back to bite him. The big one bit the underbelly of the first. When the hybrid came down, the big one attacked him in his side, slashing and digging with his tusks.

It all happened in a matter of seconds, but that was enough for both of them to get pretty bloodied up. Apparently, the bigger boar was resting and the smaller one went after him, biting him on the neck and shoulder again. The bigger boar squealed and retreated, running off without even looking back. The small, lean one trotted back to the sows and lay down on the edge in the mud like he was watching over his harem.

I was concerned that the ruckus would bring Ol' Lucifer running to the fight. From the actions of the hogs, I could tell no others were around just yet.

I sat in my foxhole watching until they wandered off. It was twilight, and I was getting cramped sitting in the hole. I felt safe—for the moment—to get out, stretch, and relieve myself away from the hole. I didn't want to leave my urine scent close to where I was. I walked about thirty feet away from the hole and relieved myself. I had been holding it for so long my bladder felt like it was going to burst.

Feeling much better and facing the fact that I had to bed down for the night in the hole, I slowly turned around scanning the shadows before total darkness set in. Nothing looked unusual until I started back for the hole. I froze in my tracks. There, coming into view from behind a small stand of shrubs, thirty feet on the other side of my foxhole, was Ol' Lucifer rooting and nosing around. He was huge and was definitely missing his right ear. He was a hauntingly beautiful specimen of a giant Russian Razorback. My initial impression was that of admiration of the beast. It didn't take long to get over it when, suddenly, he got excited and started trotting and sniffing around. He had caught my scent and trotted straight for my foxhole. I held perfectly still, hoping I wouldn't catch his attention. I felt totally helpless and stupid, regretting that I didn't keep my rifle with me. I knew better, even if it was for a few seconds. I was hoping he would wander around the wetland far enough to give me the advantage to get to my rifle. I knew he was quicker than me and if I made an attempt at getting to my foxhole right now, he would have me gored and sliced up before I could make it. I could feel my heart pumping in my throat. It was pumping so hard I thought it would give me away. I tried to slowly look around to find the nearest tree in case I had to make a run for it. He caught the motion of my head and turned to face me, taking just a moment to size me up. He snorted and I saw the hair along the ridge of his back stand straight up. I was in trouble. I didn't hesitate and made a dash for a tree that I had determined would hold me.

No sooner did I turn to run then Ol' Lucifer was on to me. I could hear and feel him coming. I was in a nightmare, moving in slow motion, not able to get away fast enough. At the edge of my life, I made it to the tree and bounced with my right leg against the tree trunk to thrust myself up so I could grab the first large branch I could reach. I pulled myself to safety, though not unscathed. Just as I grasped the branch and pulled up, Ol' Lucifer hit my left leg below the calf. I felt something snap and then an intense burn. I yanked myself into the tree, safely out of reach of the beast. He stood up, put his front hooves on the tree trunk, shaking the tree and squealed at me. He was an insanely wild animal. As large as he was, I could see every well-defined muscle in his body. I could tell he wanted me badly.

I struggled to get perched on a solid tree limb. The pain

intensified in my leg. I looked at it for the first time. Blood poured down the back of my heel, spilling onto the ground. Ol' Lucifer sniffed it and began licking it up. I groaned in pain. I carefully lifted my pant leg to see the damage. I got weak when I saw the three-inch open wound across the back of my ankle. He had completely severed my Achilles tendon leaving my foot uselessly dangling. I was shaking, growing cold from shock. I knew I would bleed to death if I didn't tie a tourniquet on my leg immediately.

I pulled out Pa's hunting knife and cut my lower pant leg off. I cut it into strips and twisted the bandage just above my ankle using a small branch. Trembling and delirious with pain, I knew I wouldn't make it through the night without toppling over, so I cut up my shirt to tie myself to the tree. I looked down and Ol' Lucifer had bedded down to wait me out. He looked content to stay there for a long time.

I tried to come up with something to scare him off. I yelled at him. He just looked up at me with his nose twitching. He snorted a few times. In the dark, he was a ghostly figure below me. I went over in my mind what survival skills I had been taught, but I found it difficult to think beyond the intense burning in my leg. The number one rule was to keep a level head and be creative.

My foot was cold and swollen and my rear was extremely sore from sitting on a branch. I knew I had to release the tourniquet every few minutes to let some blood flow or I would lose the foot entirely. Without any way back to safety, I had no idea how long this standoff would go on. In the meantime, I wondered if I would lose my foot or bleed to death trying to save it. I could see no way out. For the first time, I feared for my life. I could feel it being slowly sapped out of me. I looked down at the beast resting on his belly and looking around to scan his surroundings for other potential danger. He was the embodiment of all my fear and anger. I wanted to kill him. I focused my agony and pain on him. I had to convince myself that I would not allow Ol' Lucifer to be victorious.

In the cool of the night, the mosquitoes were eating me alive. Between the fits of burning pain that took my breath away, I would go into a swatting frenzy trying to drive the mosquitoes away. It was in vain. I didn't know at that time which would drive me insane first: the pain in my leg or the mosquitoes. The tree frogs and the cicadas were almost deafening. What used to be a soothing sound to me became a nuisance adding to my misery. Time went by so slowly. Finally, in sheer frustration, I shouted at the top of my lungs and cursed the infernal beast. He jumped to his feet, looked up, and snorted a few times. Then he rooted the ground and dug with his front hooves around him making a softer bed and lay down with his head between his front legs directly below me again. In a few minutes, he was seemingly asleep. His breathing had become regular with a loud whoosh each time he breathed out, blowing dust with each breath. Just when I thought he was down for the remainder of the night, he jumped up wide-awake snorting and grunting. He spun around like he was fighting off a band of other animals. He looked like a possessed animal tortured by his thoughts and reactions. Then as quickly as he jumped up, he lay down and was back to sleep.

For the first time, I thought of what Ma and Suzanne had told me: to turn to God. That was the only place I had to turn. At first, I turned in anger and frustration. "God, where are you? Are you going to leave me alone and empty again? Are you going to just sit back on your mighty throne and amuse yourself with my troubles, like Caesar with his gladiators? Or worse, are you going to just ignore me?

"Why is this happening God? If you're there, why is a community of good folks left to suffer from fear and dread of the unknown brought on by this beast of your creation? You made him, and he's gone wrong. Are you going to just allow him to continue aimlessly killing innocent victims? Who knows who he has tormented or killed before he came to us?" I stopped and listened to the sounds of the night, panting hard in my anger, which had turned to periodic moans of pain. I heard Ol' Lucifer's grunts.

Time passed slowly, and my anger transformed into desperate fear. I closed my eyes and tried to pray again. "Dear Lord, if you're there, and right now, I truly hope you are, I'm sorry for my earlier ranting. Please help me here. I've done all I can do and I need your help. I've been mad at you for a while now, but can you blame me? Things got purty terrible and confusin' there in 'Nam. I need to know you're there. Lord? I'm here because I'm tryin' to do the right thing—to protect the people of this community—and if there's such a thing as an evil animal spirit, this hog's got one. It's just wrong. Please help me, Lord, or I'm gonna die. I plead to you in all my humility; please help me."

When I finished, I thought about it for a while. It made me feel a little better this time. Maybe there was hope.

Chapter Eighteen

Then I thought, "The Lord helps those who help themselves." Between the throbbing pain, I tried to think of something creative. I looked at the straight branches of the cypress tree, and I had an epiphany. I needed to make a spear. I could whittle down a branch close to the trunk. I pulled out Pa's hunting knife and started whittling on the branch above me. I whittled and I prayed fervently until the branch finally broke through. I cut the little side branches off. Then, I used the last bit of my shredded shirt to tie the hunting knife to the spear. I had made a good instrument of death.

Ol' Lucifer was still just below me. I was building up the courage to throw the spear and had decided where I could do the most damage. I worked to get my good leg under me and struggled to stand up. I was really unstable after I untied myself, but I took it slow and deliberate.

I could see the sun coming up, and I dreaded the heat of the new day. I was scared to death again, but my fear had an unusual way of making me focus. I aimed to the left of his spine in the upper mid-region of his back. If I could just sink it good, he'd go off and die somewhere else. I raised the spear as high as I could with one hand holding onto a branch. I thrust it with all my force in a long hard stroke. I released the spear. It hit its mark. The knife sunk into his back. The blade only seemed to penetrate superficially compared to Ol' Lucifer's size, then it fell to his side. Ol' Lucifer let out a bloodcurdling squeal and jumped up, whirling around, snapping at whatever he could see. He bit the spear, snapping it in half.

The giant razorback ran to the water and plowed into it,

sending a spray of water ten feet high. This was my chance to get to my rifle. I climbed over to hug the tree and tried to slide down onto my good leg. I did this as quickly as I could. I almost lost my balance. I desperately clutched the tree and slid down. I hit much harder than I could support on one leg. My other foot instinctively hit the ground. The pain was excruciating. I screamed in agony. The scream caught Ol' Lucifer's attention. He spotted me on the ground, "Dear Lord, this is it," I said to myself as I crawled to get the portion of the spear that still had the knife on it.

In the second of time that I struggled with the spear, he was on me. I flinched in fear for the worst. "Crack," "Thud," it was the sound of a rifle shot and the sound of the bullet ripping through flesh. The beast's red flesh blew out the other side. Ol' Lucifer, who was almost on top of me, squealed in pain. I looked into his mouth. I could smell the death on his breath as he buckled and spun around from the impact of the bullet. He rolled onto his side, kicking and squealing. Blood spewed from the hole behind his shoulder blade and out of his mouth. As he squealed in agony, I could hear the gurgle in his lungs as they filled with blood. That moment's delay provided me the time to grab the spear. Ol' Lucifer staggered up squealing and screaming in agonizing madness and was determined to get me. I rolled over on my back with the spear pointed toward his chest and the back lodged against the tree base. I was amazed at the energy and determination of this animal after he had just been shot and had part of his insides blown out. I could see the hatred in his eyes for me as though I was the one who inflicted the pain on him. He charged me hard, screaming, with blood flying everywhere out of his mouth. He hit the spear hard, causing it to bow against the tree and impaling him deep into his chest.

"This is for my pa, my brother, and everyone else you've killed!" I screamed.

He went down flailing his razor-sharp tusks back and forth, splattering me with his blood and trying to reach me with his last bit of life. He shook and quivered as his evil spirit left his body.

I lay in total shock, amazed that I was still alive. Then, overcome with the magnitude of what had just happened, with the monster lying at my feet, I shook uncontrollably. It was over, the whole horrible ordeal was over, and I was alive to tell the story.

Chapter Nineteen

Totally exhausted and shaking, I lay at the base of the tree overwhelmed by the ordeal of the last eighteen hours.

"Who shot Ol' Lucifer? Who even knew I was back here?" I wondered to myself. Just then I heard sticks snap and leaves rustle. I jumped, fearing the ordeal was not over. In that fraction of a second, I thought the other hogs that were known to follow Ol' Lucifer were back to take over where he left off. I got up, leaning against the tree, to look and could see a man walking through the trees. Fifty feet away he came out into the open. It was Reverend Durham carrying his 30-06 rifle.

"Oh, thank the Lord, it's you!" I shouted, laughing and crying at the same time.

"Oh, so you found the Lord did you?" responded the reverend, smiling at me as he approached.

"Thank you, Lord, thank you. I'll never doubt you answer prayers again! Reverend, miracles never cease. I prayed and pleaded for help all night long and God brought you here. I cain't deny that, and you saved my life. God used you to save my life," I yelled.

"Actually, I'd put more emphasis in your Ma and Suzanne. They're the ones who came after me. Oooh! How bad's that cut on the back of your foot?" he asked.

"I think the Achilles tendon is severed. My foot's just hangin' there."

"How long you had a tourniquet on it?" the reverend asked.

"All night, but I've been bleedin' it every so often," I informed him, now panting with excitement and relief.

"We need to take it off. I hope they can save your foot. It's lookin' awful gray," he said. He immediately released the tourniquet.

"This is really gonna hurt as the circulation comes back," he said just as I screamed.

I rolled around in excruciating pain and almost fainted. He took off his shirt and tore it into bandages.

"The wound will soak these bandages, but then it'll clot. That way you'll keep circulation in your foot instead of lettin' it die from lack of oxygen," he said.

My foot burned and tingled as the circulation returned. Its pink color returned as well. The pain subsided somewhat. Now, rather than excruciating, it was intensely throbbing.

Reverend Durham walked over to inspect Ol' Lucifer. "His reign of terror is over. I just hope there ain't others like him. He's gotta be a world record; maybe worthy of the Smithsonian Institute," he marveled.

Chapter Nineteen

"You know he had five other smaller boars that used to run with him. I haven't seen any sign of 'em," I said, trying to stay in conversation and not become delirious.

"We need to get you home before this ankle gets infected and you lose that foot. Do you think you can hop if I hold you?" he asked.

"I, I can try," I said shaking and feeling very weak. Fresh blood had pooled around my ankle, but it had stopped flowing again. I tried to stand on my strong leg with the reverend's help. My leg was too weak and I felt like I was going to faint.

"Maybe I better carry you. I was able to get the truck to within a quarter mile from here. I'll leave my rifle. I really don't think anyone will come in here to steal it."

"We better take the rifle. After what I been through, I don't trust bein' without one, not even for one second," I said. With the rifle strap, I put the rifle across my back. I made my way onto his back and he tried to carry me piggyback style, but it didn't take long for him to realize my one hundred and ninety-five pounds got heavy fast.

He set me down to catch his breath. "This ain't gonna work. Maybe I need to carry you fireman style." He started to try that and couldn't even get me off the ground.

"Okay, now what?" He said as he plopped down in exhaustion.

We sat there frustrated until I spotted a couple of small dead trees.

"How about we make a stretcher and you can drag me?" I suggested as I pointed to the dead trees. He went after them and we used our remaining clothes to have something for me to lie on. By the time we were done, we were both down to our boxers and boots. I rolled on and he picked up the end. Suddenly, he sat me back down.

"We got trouble," he said looking straight ahead.

"What's the matter?" I asked, thinking he had some logistical problem. I rolled over and looked out ahead of us. The five other, smaller boars must have been drawn by the smell of blood. They now surrounded us. Quietly, and slowly, without taking his eyes off the boars, he reached down to grab the rifle. I was working to get it off me.

"I hope they're not as aggressive as Ol' Lucifer," he said. He was just going to shoot one round in the air to scatter them.

"They like human flesh as much as Ol' Lucifer, Reverend," I reminded him. He took aim and shot the biggest one of the bunch. He squealed with that horrid ree, ree, floundered around for a while, then lay still. One of the others circled around and charged us. In a single quick shot, Reverend Durham put him down too. He was an excellent shot. The last shot made the others scatter like rabbits.

"Thank goodness. I think we'd better keep our eyes open until we get to the truck," he added.

We left the boars where they were. The last thing we had on our minds was checking them out. Reverend Durham started dragging me, which still wasn't easy but it was manageable. After several rests and frustrating attempts to navigate over logs and other obstacles, we finally came within sight of the truck. I cried seeing something of civilization again. There was a point toward the end of the ordeal that I never thought I'd see anyone or anything again.

Chapter Nineteen

When we made it home, we drove by the corral. I was relieved to see Rounder made it home safely. Reverend Durham ran in the house as soon as we stopped. Ma and Suzanne came running out with the reverend behind them. They ran up to the truck door and flung it open, nearly tearing it off its hinges.

Suzanne was first to give me a big hug and about squeezed the life out of my half-delirious body anyway. "Billy, oh, Billy, I'm so glad to see you're alive. My prayers were answered."

She backed off and Ma hugged me and kissed me all over my filthy face. "You did it, Son, you got him. Hallelujah, our prayers were answered and the scourge is over." She backed off abruptly. "Oh, for heaven's sake, you're both nearly naked. Just what did happen down there?"

We all broke into laughter. It felt so good I couldn't quit laughing long enough to tell her.

Reverend Durham, now rather self-conscious said, "How does a reverend explain this one?" He smiled, then continued, "We had to use our clothes to build a stretcher for this big lug."

"Just a minute before you run to the hospital," Ma said and ran back to the house. She came back with two blankets to cover us up. We immediately took off. Ma and Suzanne called Sally, the reverend's wife, so she could bring clothes to the hospital. Then they drove to the hospital themselves.

When we got to the emergency room, the doctor took one quick look at the wound and said I needed an emergency operation or the calf muscle would contract so far that he couldn't sew it back together and I would lose the foot. In no time, the hospital staff had me under anesthesia and in the operating room, where I spent the next hour and a half. I woke up in the recovery room with five faces staring at me.

The doctor asked if I was awake enough to listen. He gave me a few minutes to become more fully aware. "Billy, we saved your foot and reattached the tendon. You'll be off this leg for quite a while and it will require extensive rehabilitation. When it's all said and done, though, I am sure you will fully recover. By the way, that was quite a story your family told me about you. As far as I'm concerned, you're quite a hero."

Reverend Durham then spoke up with Sally by his side, "I took the liberty of calling Judge McNeil and telling him Ol' Lucifer's been bagged. He literally broke into tears. He knows your family doesn't have insurance so he's going to apply the reward plus any extra to see you through to complete recovery."

That was a tremendous load off my mind. Along with the medication, I was feeling pretty good as I slipped off into a slumber.

When I awoke again, I was in a regular hospital room with Suzanne asleep on one side of the room and Ma on the other. I rolled over to look at Suzanne and realized the big cast I had on my leg. Ma and Suzanne awoke with a startle.

"You're awake. How you feelin'?" Ma asked.

"I'm just happy to be alive," I cheerfully responded.

"Me too," Suzanne responded as she stood and stretched.

"Are you hungry?" Ma asked. "The nurse was in here and I ordered you some pancakes and sausage."

"Yeah, I'm starved, but no sausage. I don't think I can eat pork ever again," I said, wrinkling my nose.

"I didn't think of that," she simply responded.

The hospital attendant brought my breakfast. It smelled heavenly. "I don't care what they say about hospital food, any food smells and tastes good right now!" I declared.

I started to eat, then I stopped. "I want to bless this food." Ma and Suzanne looked surprised, then bowed their heads to pray with me.

"Dear Lord, may we always be mindful of your hand in all things, be thankful for every day you bless us with, for our friends and loved ones both past and present, and may we be thankful for this food you abundantly bless us with. And oh, thanks for helpin' me out. Amen." I dove in to the food without looking up. When I did, I did a second take; both ladies were crying. I smiled and kept shoveling it in.

As I ate, I asked, "So, Reverend Durham said y'all were responsible for savin' me. What happened?"

Suzanne answered:

I couldn't stand it over at my friend's apartment. I missed being home, so I went back. Ma was worried into a frenzy. She came running and hugged me as soon as she heard the screen door slam. We both expressed our fear and decided to go in the living room, kneel down, and have a prayer vigil. We pleaded with God to preserve your life. No sooner did we do that then we heard a noise outside. It was

Rounder without you. We both screamed. The only person I could think of who would know how to find you was Reverend Durham. I told Ma I was going for help.

I sped as fast as your truck would let me to the reverend's house. It was almost midnight, but I didn't care. I banged on the door, and soon the reverend was there with a startled look on his face. He immediately invited me in, sensing something serious was going on. He sat me down and, by this time, Sally had joined us.

I tried to gather my wits about me and told the reverend what all you had done. I told him I feared you were dead when I saw Rounder come back with the empty saddle.

The reverend looked at his wife with deep concern. I knew from what JJ had said that he had made a commitment to his wife to not hunt hogs anymore. Without hesitation, Sally said, "May God speed." The reverend jumped up, got dressed, went for his rifle, and came home with me.

When we got home, he came in the house with me and asked a few more questions. He had only been to the spot we thought you were in one time and needed Ma to give him directions, especially since he would be driving at night.

I could see the fear in the reverend's eyes, but he took great courage and was out the door. Ma and I continued our prayer vigil into the early morning hours.

I stopped eating and lay back, taking it all in. Then I looked at both of them. "I cain't deny the Lord's hand in it all. I spent a whole night in agonizing pain with the devil of the animal world keepin' me treed. I tried to make a spear to stab the beast, but all I did was make him madder. He gave me a false hope that I could get outta the tree and back to my gun when he ran to a pond. I fell from the tree and screamed in agonizing pain, which just got Ol' Lucifer's attention again. I'm here to tell you, if it hadn't been for a miracle, that beast would've cut me up into little pieces. He charged me and just when I was lookin' in the mouth of the beast, Reverend Durham shot him. That gave me the seconds I needed to get my spear again. Ol' Lucifer raised himself up and came at me again with blood spewin' from his side and outta his mouth. Flat on the ground, I held fast to that spear and that mighty beast impaled himself right before me. I'm tellin' you it was a miracle I cain't deny."

Ma and Suzanne were in tears, marveling and smiling at the same time.

"Mornin', folks." We turned; it was the doctor. "I see y'all are doing a lot better this mornin'. How are you feeling, young man?"

"I'm doin' great and just glad to be alive!" I answered.

"Would you like to go home to recover?" asked the doctor.

"Yessir, I sure would," I happily replied.

"Well, if you can make it through the barrage of reporters and camera people waiting in the lobby for you, then you can go home. Your story has been all over the news," the doctor cheerfully warned.

Later, the nurse came in and helped me into a wheel-chair. Suzanne pushed me down to the loading area. When we got to the lobby, the photographers started flashing, and the news cameras rolled.

"Hello, Billy Longbow. How does it feel to be the hero of Lufkin?" shouted one of the reporters. I had five micro-phones in my face.

I threw my arms in the air and said, "I'm happy to be alive, and I thank God for another day."

Just then, the crowd parted and Judge McNeil stepped forward, "Billy Longbow, on behalf of my family first and foremost and on behalf of this community, I want to thank you for your meritorious bravery. Rural families, espe-cially, will rest easier because of your actions. You have done this community a great honor and have set an example to all of us in giving your life to the service of your fellow citizens through your recent service in Vietnam and in showing the same bravery here. Again, thank you." He stepped forward to shake my hand and the cameras flashed again.

I hadn't thought about it until now, but in some small way, I felt redeemed from the weight of the guilt I felt for not being there fighting with my buddies to the end in Vietnam. I was able to let go and realize God had preserved me for another time.

Ma had just pulled up with the truck. Suzanne helped me get in. I sat in the middle and draped my casted leg over into Suzanne's spot. When we were driving off, I turned to Ma, "There's somewhere I want to go before we go home."

"Billy, don't you think we ought to just get you home so you can rest?" replied Ma.

I glanced at Suzanne. She looked puzzled. I looked back at Ma. "No, this is important. Take me to Mrs. Guseman's home."

"You mean the lady whose husband was attacked by that hog when he was trying to help JJ?" asked Ma.

"Yep, that's the one," I replied. "I got somethin' to give her."

I saw Ma look down at the key chain with the gold ring hanging on it. "Yeah, Ma, I want to return something that belongs to her."

She smiled and turned the other direction from home.

We got to the Guseman's home and, along with my crutches, Suzanne helped me to the door. I felt anxious as I rang the doorbell. I had no idea how we would be received.

The door opened and a sweet-looking, little Hispanic lady answered the door. "Can I help you?" One of her daughters, who looked about fourteen, stood behind her.

"Uh, yes, ma'am. My name is Billy Longbow and I came to return somethin' that belongs to you."

"Oh! You're Billy! Yes, now I recognize you. You are the one on the news. You killed that devil hog that..." Her chin started to quiver.

"I, uh, just wanted to tell you I'm sorry about Stephen. I just wanted to return this to you," and I handed her the wedding ring.

She looked at it, graciously took it, and put it on her middle finger. In a burst of tears, she reached up and gave me a hug. She hugged me for a long time, and I could feel her sobbing on my shoulder.

"Thank you, Billy. Thank you for bringing some closure to our family's grief. You are a hero in our home. We will always grieve the loss of my sweet husband. We were not getting along. I was mean to him. I kicked him out of our home. He loved me. And I really did love him. Now I will never be able to tell him so." She pulled back. "Oh, I'm sorry. I didn't mean to burden you." She sniffed, straightened up. "God bless you," she said giving me an endearing look.

"He already has more than you can imagine," I replied.

Her daughter then came forward. "Thank you, sir," she said bashfully, but with a smile. I nodded and smiled back at her.

"God bless you folks too," I said, turned around and hobbled back to the truck. Feeling good, I looked at Suzanne when we got to the truck door. "Let's go home, Suzanne."

She smiled that beautiful smile at me and opened the door. "Get in, cowboy."

Epilogue

Over thirty years later, I sit on this train, a month after starting my book, and put the completing touches to it. It took many late night hours to get it written.

It causes me to reflect on how things have changed since then. My foot is healed, but my heel still bothers me on cold days. I still walk with a mild limp from the gunshot wound I received in Vietnam.

By the end of that summer, I enrolled at the Stephen F. Austin College in Nacogdoches in the school of journalism. Eventually, I finished my education at the University of Texas in Austin. I had a long way to go to get rid of my East Texas slang. Now, I am an editor for the widest circulated newspaper in the metroplex.

Reverend Durham called the Smithsonian Institute to tell them of what he thought was the world's largest Black Russian Razorback and perhaps literally the largest member of the suidae or hog family. I was satisfied to never see the beast again. As far as I was concerned, his friends could make a meal out of him.

When the zoologists representing the Smithsonian saw the giant, they were beside themselves with excitement. They said Ol' Lucifer was a genetic wonder and were going to do a chromosome study to find out if he was the product of an unusual hybrid vigor or an unusual strain of rare giant hogs. They said they had read legends about hogs like this before. The legends were hidden in the annals of Russian royalty.

The men were very impressed when they saw the spear still stuck in the boar's chest. They knew there was a good story to be shared historically. They joked about how it reminded them of the way cavemen obtained food. I didn't see the humor. They asked me to write down my story. At the time, I never wanted to relive that experience again. Now, I realize this story is part of our East Texas legacy and keeps Pa and JJ alive in the minds and hearts of our children.

As for Jonas, the Cajun giant was released from the hospital with a clean bill of health. He became a common scene around the ranch. He sold his place in Zapalla and moved to Lufkin. With me being gone so much, he pretty much became Ma's third son and helps her take care of the ranch.

Later that summer, I took Suzanne with me to South Padre Island and spent a few days in the sun on the beach. I was still in my cast, but I didn't mind the scenery— watching Suzanne in her swimsuit chasing the waves and helping a couple little kids build a sand castle. There, on the beach at sunset, watching the waves come and go with Suzanne beside me in her lounge chair, we talked.

"I've felt so much a part of your family even before the sad turn of events," she said, smiling at me.

I thought about how comfortable I had always been with her. "Do you know how much I love you?" I boldly asked.

"Yes, I think so, and I love you so much. I just feel like you're a part of me," she responded.

"Suzanne?" I paused making sure I had her full attention, "Will you marry me an' spend the rest of your life with me?"

"Yes, oh yes!" she screamed. "I thought you were never going to ask me." She jumped up and dived on me, giving me a big hug and collapsing my lounge chair. We laughed and hugged. Other people watching joined in the laughter. I think they caught on to what was happening as they listened to Suzanne's screams of joy.

We were married the end of August just before school started. Suzanne understood my abhorrence for crowds and agreed to a quaint wedding in that little white church I had grown up in. Reverend Durham proudly married us. When we said, "I do," we began what still is a long and happy marriage. Ma hugged Suzanne on our way out the church door and said she had prayed for this day, and she couldn't have asked for a better daughter.

Reflecting on my years now and the events of my life, I've come to know that we do have the ability to change events; that everything isn't just total randomness. Now in my later years, I know God hears the petitions and intense prayers of his godly, earnest children. I believe my mother's prayers saved me in Vietnam, at home, and kept Suzanne and me together; and I believe he heard one man's earnest prayer in the bowels of the Angelina River bottoms that lonely night over thirty years ago.

Now, with that traumatic summer far behind us—although occasionally I still relive those times in my dreams—life is good. We have four beautiful children starting families of their own; Mattie our youngest, Kurt, Ashley, and our eldest son, Jack the third. The memory of my pa and brother lives on.

Acknowledgments

I would like to express my appreciation to all those who encouraged me to write this book. After watching me write three other books (which incidentally are forthcoming), my son Bryan asked me to write a horror book. I told him it wasn't my nature to write horror books. "Ah, come on, Dad, just one," was his persistent response to me. I told him that I did not want horror books to be the genre I was known for, that I was more of an adventure writer.

I thought that was the end of it, until one day I visited the Big Brown Lignite Mining Area, in east central Texas, as part of my job. There, in the mining office, was a bust of a huge black razorback hog. It had its mouth wide open with tusks four inches long and an angry look in its eyes. I commented on how vicious this animal looked. Being originally from Utah, I was unfamiliar with wild/feral hogs. The old seasoned cowboys, employees of the mine, started telling me stories of their experiences, and experiences of their friends, who had crossed paths with angry hogs. It is a big pastime in East Texas to hunt these hogs on horseback with dogs, and capture them alive for export to other countries for food.

One of my now good friends told me he had been to Vietnam as a side-gunner on a helicopter and he has never been so scared as when a big hog tried to run him down. He saved himself by diving over a creek bed, grabbing a tree limb, and climbing to safety. He said the hog kept him treed for nearly ten minutes before losing interest and wandering off. He also told me of a local football coach—a big man and avid hunter—who had been killed by hogs. He has since guided me, climbing and hiking through the hog's habitat, to observe them and learn more about their resilient and opportunistic nature. This story, and many others I have since heard, convinced me that there was a good story to be told here. I can proudly say I enjoyed writing this book, not as a horror, but as a compelling thriller. Of course now my son takes full credit for the book.

I also want to express my appreciation to my editor, Norlan De Groot, for his tireless efforts and true professionalism in editing the book; and the cover designers for helping me provide a top-notch product that I can be proud of and others can enjoy for years to come.

About the Author

The author, Scott Wilde, grew up in northern Utah with the Rocky Mountains and their vast resources as his playground. Scott graduated from Utah State University with a degree in geology and worked as a geophysicist for a major petroleum exploration company for several years. As a husband and father of seven children, he now lives in Granbury, Texas, and works for a leading electric company as an environmental specialist. He shares his love for the outdoors with his family and other youth through his activities as a seasoned backpacker, scoutmaster, and through his love of writing. His family, and those who associate with him, has always enjoyed his stories and now he shares one of his favorite thriller stories through his first published book, *Razorback*.